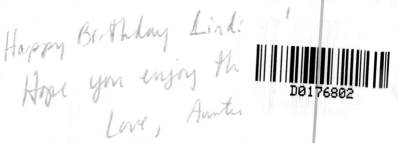

Happy Birthday Lind:
Hope you enjoy th
Love, Aunt

Julie the Brave

The Discovery

CORINNE MAGID

ISBN-13: 978-1503336407
ISBN-10: 1503336409

To Makyla, Aubrey, Cole and Amelia

I gathered a piece of each of your souls and held them close to my heart. Then I mixed them together to make a potion and poured it into the recipe that made Julie Everbeam. Thank you for all your ideas. I love you.

CHAPTER 1

Once upon a time, there lived a girl named Jules Everbeam, but everyone called her Julie. She was ten years old with long ordinary brown hair and bright blue eyes. She felt ordinary in every single way, except for one. For most of her life, Julie felt like she was waiting. She'd wake up on the floor in that gray room where she slept with her three younger brothers, listening to their slow breaths as they slept. She'd open one eye, and just for a second, she'd hope that maybe things had changed. Maybe, she'd wake up in a bed wearing a new dress and she'd smell breakfast cooking in the kitchen. But then she'd open her other eye and look around the room. She'd give a little sigh when she saw she still slept on the floor in that tiny drafty room, with a thin gray blanket that never kept her warm. She still had on that tired gray dress with the unraveling hem. And of course, she woke up with that grumbling in her tummy and dreams of soft delicious bread.

Julie lived a long, long time ago in a land far, far away. A time before cars and phones and most everything that made life easy. You see, Julie's life was very hard. It was hard, not because Julie's parents didn't love her. Oh, they loved her so very much. They gave her kisses and hugs whenever they could. Her father was the first one to lift her in the air and twirl her around. Her mother gave her soft hugs and whispered words about how life would get better soon. But it never did. Her parents tried to give her all the love they could because love was free. You see, Julie's parents tried to find enough work to feed their four children, but they always came up short.

So on this particular day, Julie woke up and opened one eye. She saw her seven-year-old brother Sam sleeping next to her peacefully with his arms outstretched, taking way more than his share of the floor. She opened the other eye and saw her four-year-old brother Jacob and two-year-old brother Benjamin sleeping with the big blanket

Julie had long given up to them to keep them warm at night. Julie heard the grumbling in her tummy so loud she sat up and looked at those gray walls and her gray dress and decided to do something about it.

For three nights in a row, Julie told her mother she did not want her dinner porridge. Even if it wouldn't be enough to fill her tummy, Julie still refused. Her mother knew what Julie was doing. Julie gave up her dinner so her brothers could eat more. Julie went to bed so very hungry that night. Without her brothers noticing, she cried and cried until her pillow was wet. She told herself she'd take just that one night to feel sorry for herself. Then in the morning, if nothing changed by the time she woke up, she would do something about it.

Well, tomorrow arrived with the dawn peeking through the dusty window. As Julie opened both eyes, she realized nothing had changed. She sat up, threw on her shoes and started her day.

Today, Julie was done waiting.

CHAPTER 2

Julie decided to look for a job. She set out on this particular day after a hug from her mother wishing her good luck. As she walked down the big busy street past carriages and horses, Julie looked up at the sun peeking through the gloomy clouds and thought about what she might do for work. Julie didn't go to school because school in Julie's town cost money and Julie had no money. But Julie's mother taught Julie her letters and how to read and write. Knowing how to read was more than most poor girls and so Julie hoped it might help her find a job. But then she thought about how her mama and papa could read and write, and they were grownups and couldn't find enough work. She started to get sad in her heart and almost decided to give up, but the grumbling in her tummy kept her going.

Julie walked for about an hour before she passed a big beautiful house with flowering trees growing outside. Two ladies in pretty gowns walked out the front door and stepped into a lovely carriage.

"Maybe I could clean their house for them," Julie said to the roses outside trying to keep her spirits up. "Rich ladies don't want to spend time cleaning. They might get their gowns dirty."

Julie watched the carriage leave, then walked up to the front door, smoothed her gray dress, and stood up straight. She reached up to the gold knocker and knock, knock, knocked on the door. A maid in a crisp white dress with her hair pinned neatly behind her head answered the door.

"What do we have here?" the maid snarled, looking down at Julie from her very pointy nose. "What's a street rat like you doing in this neighborhood?"

Julie felt her lip quiver as she tried not to cry. She almost ran away, but took a deep breath and tried to sound grown up. "I'm... well... I'm wondering if you need any help here cleaning this grand house. I am a very hard worker and I could help—"

"I'd never hire you!" The maid sneered. Julie thought interrupting was very bad manners and wondered how a maid with such bad manners could work in such a fancy house. She didn't say anything because she felt too stunned to speak. "You'd steal all our silver and never work a day! Now get out of here you dirty girl before I call for the police!"

With those nasty words, the maid slammed the door in Julie's face. Julie worried the police might try and take her away, so she ran as fast as she could from those fancy houses. Julie didn't give herself the chance to cry even though she wanted to. After all, her brothers needed food and crying on the curb wouldn't feed her brothers.

Once she got out of the neighborhood, she walked down a busy bustling street and smelled the delicious smell of bread. It curled into her nose, leading her to the baker around the corner. Sometimes, when Julie felt extra hungry, she sat outside the bakery and smelled the bread and imagined what it would be like to eat just one delicious roll. She'd done that when she was nine years old, but now she was ten and ready to work.

Julie thought about the hard work it must be for the baker to make all that bread. He had to roll out the dough, put the bread in the oven, help customers, and clean the floor. Julie smiled at what an excellent idea it was to try and work at the bakery. The baker could pay her in bread! Julie wasn't quite as nervous as she had been at the grand house because she felt so excited at the thought of bringing home a warm loaf of bread for her brothers to eat every day.

Julie went to the back door so the baker didn't have to worry about his customers seeing a girl in a sad gray dress in the front of his store. She took a deep breath and knocked. It took just a moment for the baker to open the door. He was a big fat man dressed in an apron with mean eyes and a mouth that never smiled. He held one of his delicious rolls and chomped a bite as he glared at her.

Before he could say anything, Julie blurted out her speech. "Mr. Baker. My name is Julie. I am a very hard worker and want to ask you for a job. You could pay me in bread and I could sweep your floor and clean your bakery and roll dough and help make your life easier." Julie felt quite proud of herself on how grown up she sounded. She didn't tell him she was only ten. She hoped he might think she was older.

The baker snorted. "Get out of here!" he yelled with his mouth full of bread, sending crumbs flying into Julie's hair. Again, Julie thought he had very bad manners to talk with his mouth full, but she didn't point this out to him. She needed the job. "If I gave you a job, you would eat all my bread. I can tell from your hungry eyes you haven't had a good meal in a very long time. Now stay away from my bakery and don't bother me again!"

With that, the baker slammed the door in Julie's face. This time, she felt more angry than hurt. He was just like that maid, so rude to slam a door. After all, she was just a little girl asking for work. She didn't understand why he needed to act so mean.

Julie shook the crumbs from her hair as she walked away from the bakery. She felt very concerned her day was not working out as she had hoped. She crossed her arms around her grumbling tummy so she didn't have to hear the rumbles and walked right down the street. An old woman with wild hair and even more wild eyes saw Julie, hobbled up to her, and grabbed her arm.

"You need work child?" The woman gripped a bit too tight on Julie's arm and put her face so close, Julie could smell the lady's breath. It smelled like rotten rubbish and Julie shuddered. "Then go to that factory over there. They'll take most everyone if you can handle it." The old woman cackled and pointed a finger full of warts to a door down a dark alley.

The alley was so dark that Julie could barely see a brown door down the stairs to a basement. The woman let go and Julie took slow steps toward the alley. It wasn't that she was afraid of the dark exactly, but it was terribly dark down there. She glanced back at the old woman and considered turning around and sprinting home. But then she thought about her brothers eating porridge again that night and gulped down her fear. She mustered enough courage to walk into the shadows and down the stairs to that dark door.

Before she had a chance to knock, she heard a man inside the door yelling, "Go faster! No, you can't have water! You mustn't stop! I don't care if you need to go to the bathroom!" Julie did not like this man's voice and she thought it was very rude not to let someone use the bathroom when they needed it, but she decided to knock, knock, knock on the door and see if that yelling voice would pay her to work.

"What do you want!?!" yelled the voice.

Because the voice sounded so mean, Julie thought the voice came from a giant of a man. But as the door swung open, in front of her stood a man not much taller than her. He wore a purple velvet suit that was sweaty from the heat drifting from the room. He was out of breath from his yelling and stood there with his hands on his hips, daring Julie to speak. Julie did not appreciate his tone of voice, but decided it was best to ignore it and just ask for a job.

"What do I want?" Julie answered. She sounded more and more grown up each time she had to ask, "I'd like a job."

The little man looked her over from top to bottom and then snatched up her hand. He looked at her hand for a very long time measuring her hand against his. "Nope, won't do child. Your hands are far too little for what I need in my factory." He dropped her hand and grabbed the door. "Come back when you are twelve. Maybe then I'll take you in. Until then, stop wasting my time!"

With those words, another door slammed in Julie's face. Julie slumped on the stair outside the door and hugged her arms around her knees. For just a bit, she let her head rest on the cold brick wall. If she couldn't get a job where a mean little man yelled and screamed, then where would she find work? She was learning some adults could be terribly rude.

Julie decided she'd had far too much disappointment for the day. She wasn't exactly giving up, but a girl can only take so many insults in one day. She had a long walk home, so she stood up and brushed herself off. Then she covered her tummy to quiet the grumbling and walked down the busy main street of her town.

She almost made it home when the rain started. It started as a few drip drops, but as she walked further to the edge of town to her house, the rain clouds opened up and just dumped rain on her. She could have handled the rain if it wasn't for the great big windstorm that started. The rain pelted her face as the wind rushed against her, making it impossible to even walk. Then the wind shifted. It felt like it pushed her not toward her house, but into another dark alley. Julie tried to fight the wind, but it blew against her face and whipped her hair.

She squinted down the alley and saw that it wasn't much darker than the one she had just visited. So she decided to wait for the storm to stop before she went home. She walked down that alley and then a big gust of wind swirled up around her and thumped her right into a huge red door. Just as her feet hit the welcome mat, the wind stopped. As Julie turned to walk back into the street, something caught her eye. The big red door shimmered like a rainbow filled with glitter.

"Impossible," Julie whispered and shook her head. She stared back at the door and blinked. She thought maybe her hungry tummy was playing tricks on her mind because for just one second, she thought she had seen the words, "*Julie, Please Knock*" written in the glitter. She rubbed her eyes and the words disappeared.

CHAPTER 3

Julie sat down on the stoop right next to that shimmering door and stared at it. She rubbed her eyes and looked away, then looked back again. The rain and wind had stopped, so Julie could watch the door without much trouble. She could have sworn she had seen her name on the door, but then again that was crazy.

"Miss Door," Julie said in her grown up voice she had practiced all morning. Julie just knew by the colors of that door it had to be a girl. "I do appreciate your very good manners of saying please, but how in the world do you know my name?"

The door rewarded Julie for asking a question by turning a brilliant purple. Purple just happened to be Julie's favorite color.

"Miss Door, I've had a very terrible day and I'm wondering if you could tell me if there is work inside this house. I am looking for work so I can help my little brothers." The door flashed gold, orange, then blue. A shiver ran up Julie's spine because those three colors were her brothers' favorite colors. She blinked and tried to use her best grown up face to hide her surprise.

"Miss Door, before I knock on you, I must know one thing." Julie put her hands on her hips just like that little man from the factory so she looked like a boss. "I need to know that if I knock, the person who opens you isn't going to yell at me and tell me to go away. I very much feel that I would not appreciate that."

The door turned into the colors of a glitter rainbow. Then a door knocker appeared in the shape of a dolphin with a blooming plumeria flower on its tail. It stood the perfect height for Julie.

"Well Miss Door, I guess it doesn't hurt to knock," Julie said. As she reached for the door knocker, she felt the door give off a little shiver. If she hadn't known more about doors, she would have thought it smiled. Julie gave that door a knock, knock, knock and waited for someone to open it.

CHAPTER 4

Julie felt her heart thump in her chest. The thumping matched her breath shaking from her. Julie liked this door and hoped she didn't belong to some big meanie like those other places she had visited today. She would very much like to work in a place where the door smiled at her every time she came to work.

Just as Julie almost lost her nerve and walked away, the door opened with a slow scary creak. There in front of her, stood a very old woman. The woman wore her long gray hair tied in a bun, with one shining gold strand growing near her face. She stood stooped and leaning on a cane made of a twisted purple tree branch. After Julie had such a terrible scare from that old woman in the street, Julie expected this woman to smell of rubbish too. Instead, the smell of honeysuckle floated from the doorway. Two cats wove between the woman's feet. One was the color of night and the other the color of snow. Julie had the odd feeling the white cat winked at her. She remembered that it wasn't polite to stare, so she cleared her throat and stood up straight.

"Hello, I'd like to ask you for a job," Julie said simply.

The old woman looked at Julie with one blue eye and one green. She smiled and then handed Julie a loaf of bread. Julie stood stunned holding the bread in her palms.

"Julie, I've waited ten years for you to arrive," the old woman said. "You really left us wondering if you'd ever come at all."

"Us?" Julie whispered, looking at the bread and wondering if it was a trick. Her questions tumbled out before she could decide if she should run. "How do you know my name? Why were you waiting for me? How could I come here if I never knew you existed?"

"Oh Julie, all of us have been waiting, especially your Aunt Cora." The old woman looked a bit tired by Julie's questions. "I'll explain, don't worry. First, a proper introduction. This is Madam Doorika. Madam Doorika is, well, she's a door. My name is Emerald and I am a witch."

"A witch!" Julie gasped and took a step back, almost tumbling off the steps. She considered running away with the bread, but wondered if the witch would hop on a broom and chase after her. She'd heard stories of witches eating little kids and being overall very bad. She wanted to run, but her grumbling tummy told her to stay.

"Oh yes," Emerald sighed. "I'm sure you have heard all sorts of tales of nasty witches. Plus your Aunt Cora hasn't been here to explain the truth. Let's sit down for a bit. We can talk while we eat. That grumbling stomach of yours is a bit too noisy for me to think right now." Emerald sighed and gave her cane a little wave in the air. Two little chairs magically appeared outside in the alley.

"Um... okay," Julie mumbled, covering her stomach with her hands. "Sorry about my tummy."

"Not a problem my dear," Emerald waved her hand. "It's nothing a little magic can't fix right up."

With another wave of her cane, a table appeared with two tall glasses of milk. Julie's tongue tingled at the thought of that cold milk sliding down her throat. The bread flew out of Julie's hands, sliced itself and landed on two plates. Julie sat down and tried to figure out what to do. Her parents had warned her never to take food from strangers. But as scared as she thought she should be of witches, she was even hungrier. Julie picked up that delicious milk and tried to politely drink it, but the moment it touched her tongue, she gulped it down. Then she took a slice of bread and took a tiny bite, letting it rest at the tip of her tongue. She tried not to snatch the rest off her plate and shove it in her mouth, but it was banana bread with bits of butter. She sighed with delight and finished it off in two giant bites. Once she finished, a napkin appeared and wiped her face, then floated down to her lap. She was just about to use her best manners to ask for another slice of bread, when two slices flew onto her plate.

"Aren't witches mean?" Julie blurted out between bites. She wasn't sure if it was bad manners to ask, but she really wanted to know if she was going to get turned into a toad or something.

"Oh no, child," Emerald smiled. Julie felt relieved Emerald had all her teeth. Her smile was kind and not at all scary for a witch. "Most of us are very nice. There are some grumpy ones, and some are mean, but overall witches are very nice people. There was a time when people would come to witches all the time and bother us for this spell and that spell. 'Please make this girl fall in love with me.' 'Make me the richest person in the world.' 'Make me queen right now.' You know, that sort of thing."

Julie nodded as if she knew, but she'd never heard of anyone knowing a witch to even ask for those things.

"Most of the time, people did not say please or even thank you and it took all of a witch's time just to tend to the people asking for silly help. So we got together and started the stories of all those evil witches. We got very creative and finally we had some peace and quiet."

Julie bit her lip. "But how do I know if a witch is mean?" she asked. She thought this was a good question to figure out if Emerald planned to cook her in a pot of witch's brew.

"You would know a mean witch from the moment you looked into her eyes." Emerald shuttered and pushed away whatever bad memory had floated into her mind. "But those stories are for another day. As for you, your mother has never told you about Cora?"

"My mama told me she has a twin named Cora," Julie answered trying to seem helpful, but she felt more and more confused.

"Julie, your Aunt Cora is a witch, a very powerful and good witch."

"Ohhhh," Julie said, but her mouth stayed open until she remembered the bread squished between her teeth and so she closed her mouth with a snap.

"And Julie, you are a witch too."

Julie gulped and the silence curled around them. "What? I… no… that's impossible." Julie finally stammered.

"It's not impossible, it's the truth. On the day you were born, your Aunt Cora wrote to me. She said the greatest witch anyone had ever seen had been born to her sister. Cora was so delighted. She said she planned to train you as a witch as soon as you could talk. But Cora was called away to a far away land to protect others from an evil wizard. She's been there ever since. She told me someday your mother would bring you here to train. I've waited for that day ever since."

"But my mother isn't a witch." Julie knew this for sure. If her mother was a witch, surely they would've eaten something better than porridge every night for the last year.

"Yes, that's true. That's why you are so special. A witch born to a human is very rare. Cora loves her twin so very much, but they could not be more different. When Cora left, she asked your mother to train you as a witch. Your mother said you had done nothing magical. She said if you showed any magical talent then maybe she would send you here. She wanted you to have a normal childhood. Not a childhood filled with potions and magic spells like her sister's."

"But I'm not magical," Julie said through bites of her fourth piece of bread. If she had magical powers, she would have flown into that bakery today and taken a big bowl of flour and dumped it onto the mean baker, then flown straight to her family with all those rolls. If she was a witch, her family would have a warm dinner every night.

Emerald smiled. "Oh child, I can tell by the way you sit that you have more magic in the tip of your nose, than I could hope to have in a lifetime."

Julie didn't think that could be true, but she wiggled her nose just in case. Nothing happened, but she liked this Emerald. Emerald made her feel special. Emerald reached into her pocket and pulled out a green and yellow necklace made of seashells. She handed it to Julie.

"Take this necklace to your mother and show it to her. She will know it is Cora's because Cora wore it every day as a child." Julie slipped the necklace on. She liked the way the necklace hummed against her skin, feeling like it whispered hello to her. "Once your mother has seen it, tell her I'd like you to come here and train every day."

Julie felt her heart fall. She really needed to work to feed her family and she couldn't train as a witch if she had a job.

"Thank you very much for the offer." Julie took a sad look around the little alley and sighed. "But I need a job. I can't come here."

"Tell your mother I will pay you in food," Emerald said. "Soon enough you will be able to make your own food." With another wave of her cane, Emerald handed Julie three loaves of bread. "Now go to your house child, and come back in the morning."

Julie's face felt too small for the great big smile that spread across it. She thanked Emerald over and over again. Then she stacked those three loaves of bread into her arms and ran home as fast as she could. She ran because she couldn't wait to show her brothers her treasures, but she also ran because she was afraid Emerald would change her mind and steal the bread away right before she turned Julie into a toad.

CHAPTER 5

When Julie reached her house at the end of a gravel road, she flung open the door and burst into the kitchen where her family sat around the table ready to split one bowl of porridge between them all.

"Look!" Julie shouted as she held her arms wide to show the bread. Her mother gasped and her brothers squealed. Her father picked her up and swung her around and around. They all giggled and laughed as Julie sliced the bread onto the plates they hadn't used in a very long time.

Julie handed the bread slices to her brothers. Her baby brother Benjamin squished the bread up against his face, buried his mouth into it and took big gulping bites. Her four-year-old brother Jacob took the tiniest bites, so slow the bread melted in his mouth. Her seven-year-old brother Sam muttered while he ate and patted his tummy saying, "So yummy Julie, so yummy." Julie smiled sweetly at him and decided not to tell him it was bad manners to talk with his mouth full because he looked so happy. Her parents said they weren't hungry, but Julie sliced the bread for them anyway and finally they each took a plate.

Her mother pushed her slice of bread around her plate without eating it, then looked up at Julie with worried eyes. "Where did you get the bread?" her mother asked in a hushed voice.

"I'll tell you later," Julie whispered. Her mother nodded, but looked as if she swallowed the questions that sat on the tip of her tongue.

After they ate and packed away the leftover loaf for the next day, the whole family sat around making each other laugh. Julie couldn't remember the last time they laughed so hard all together. She stared at her giggling family and her heart felt so happy she thought it might burst. After they settled down and it was time for bed, Julie's mother asked Julie to walk outside with her.

They walked along a stone path outside their house. The moon was pinned in the sky like a half smile. Julie grabbed her mother's hand. Julie was not too old to still enjoy taking walks with her mother and now she looked at her mother and beamed. Her heart felt so free. Her mother smiled back as she brushed her long brown hair out of her green eyes.

Julie squeezed her mother's hand in their secret code. Julie squeezed two quick squeezes. Her mother answered back in three squeezes of her own. Her mother always said it was her silent way of saying she loved Julie more than she could ever understand. When they reached a big oak tree, they stopped and sat down on the grass.

"Julie, that was a very grand gift you gave us today," said her mother. She sat quiet for awhile, then shifted to look Julie in the eyes. "How did you get that bread?" When Julie didn't answer she whispered, "did you steal it?"

"No, of course not," Julie answered, but her mother's words stung. She would never steal, but she didn't want to think about what she might have done if she hadn't met Emerald. "Cora's friend Emerald gave it to me," she said.

"Cora's friend?" Julie's mother's voice shook. "Your Aunt Cora?"

"Yes Mama."

"Julie, did Emerald say anything… peculiar?"

"Not peculiar Mama. She told me the most wonderfully brilliant things." Julie took a deep breath and the words tumbled out. "She said Cora is a witch and I am a witch and that she would train me to be a better witch. Mama if I train as a witch, she will give us food! She said I could learn to make food for us! That I am magical!" Julie flopped back into the grass and stared at the sky with her cheeks rosy as she laughed. She looked up at her mother to share in a smile. Her mother smiled, but her eyes looked scared. Julie sat up and her mother saw the hint of the necklace peeking out of Julie's dress.

"What is it Mama?"

Her mother reached up with shaking hands and touched the necklace around Julie's neck. "Did Emerald give this to you?"

"Do you remember it?" Julie whispered. "Emerald said Cora wore it as a little girl. Mama, what is it? Why aren't you happy?" Julie pressed her hands against her mother's trembling hand.

"I do not like this Julie." Her mother pulled her close. Her tears rolled into Julie's hair. "I do not like this at all." She let out a shuttering breath.

"Yes, my sister Cora is a witch, a witch weighed down by what she thinks she must do. She stopped being a little girl once she learned about her magic when we were ten. Even though we were just children, she had to grow up and stop acting like a little girl."

"How Mama?" Julie pressed her face into her mother's shoulder. She forgot sometimes that her mother had a life before she was born. It was hard to think of her as anything but a mother.

"On our tenth birthday, a witch named Ruby marched up to our door and told our mother that Cora was a witch. Ruby said Cora must fulfill her destiny and train her magic." Julie's mother lifted the sleeve of her dress to show her wrist. "I should have known. Even though we were twins, Cora was born with a silver star on her left wrist. That star was the only way anyone could tell us apart. When Ruby arrived, Cora stopped playing and started working every day. Ruby said I was too much of a distraction to help and so we barely saw each other after that."

"Was it always bad?" Julie held her breath.

"No, we had fun when Ruby wasn't around," her mother smiled, lost in the memory. "Once, Cora accidentally cast a spell that made one hundred baby bunnies appear in our house. We'd sit down at the table and a bunny would hop out from under our cushions. I once found five snuggled up on my pillow before bed. It took us months to finally find them all. Another time, Cora wanted to make us a chocolate cake, but she got the spell wrong and our entire bedroom filled with one big cake smashing us against the walls. We had to eat a tunnel to get out of the room. It took a week for me to finally get all the frosting out of my hair."

Julie giggled, imagining her mother as a little girl covered in cake from head to toe.

"Mostly though, she worked. Ruby was always at our house, never letting Cora play. At least at night we could sit in the room we shared together and fall asleep after we talked. But one day, when we were twelve, Ruby told Cora she had to fly to a faraway place to help fight the Darkness. Weeks later, Cora returned. She flew through a terrible storm into our bedroom window, soaking and trembling with fear. She was a different girl after that. Whatever she saw, it changed her." Julie's mama hugged Julie tighter.

"What did she see?" Julie whispered.

"I don't know. She never told me. That night, as I hugged her, she just kept repeating, 'the Darkness crept out and I stopped it.' But she refused to tell me what happened. Afterwards, it was as if she followed a destiny she didn't want. She never let herself rest. Her fight to help others never ended. She left on her latest quest when we were twenty four. She has been gone now for ten years. Ten years, Julie!"

Julie touched her mom's cheek and a tear slid down Julie's finger into her hand. Julie looked at it and it shimmered green, her mother's favorite color. It rolled in Julie's hand like a ball. Julie put the tear in her dress pocket. She didn't know why she wanted to save it, but she did.

"Julie, you don't even know her. Your brothers don't even know her. It breaks my heart not to see my twin sister for ten years, but if I didn't see you for ten years my heart would turn black." Her mother brushed off the tears from her face and looked into Julie's eyes. "Before she left, she told me you were a great witch and that I had to work to make you stronger. But why would I do that to you? Why would I ever train you for something that might hurt you? My job is to protect you, my love. Not to send you to someone who will steal your childhood and make you afraid."

"Mama, we need the food." Julie said it quietly as she burrowed her face into her mother's hair. Julie's mother squeezed her eyes shut. Julie didn't want to argue, but they both knew she was right.

"I know, my sweet. I know." Her mother blinked her tears from her eyes and sighed. "You must go. It is what you were born to do. You are right, we need the food and I am in no place to say no. I hope this Emerald will teach you how to take care of yourself before she asks you to fight the Darkness."

Julie hugged her mother and they sat quiet for a long time just listening to the breeze singing through the trees. Finally, Julie mustered up enough courage to speak.

"So can I train as a witch?" she said in a tiny voice.

"You can go. But you must promise me that if it starts to get too scary, you will stop. Do you promise?"

"Yes Mama. I promise."

"And I promise to guard you from the Darkness if I can," Julie's mother said. "I promise to always try and protect you."

Julie watched the words of their promises turn to a mist that then tied itself together with a red bow. The promises floated up into the haze of the sky. That day, Julie had felt so very grown up to have found food for her family. But as the words reached the clouds, Julie no longer felt grown up. She felt very much like she was just ten years old and too young for what life had in store for her.

CHAPTER 6

The next day, Julie woke up and opened both eyes at the same time. Her brother Sam still took up way too much of the floor and she still shivered without a blanket. Her dress still didn't keep her warm in that drafty room. No delicious breakfast smell floated in from the kitchen, but the sun felt like it danced from inside her. Julie smiled. Yes, her mother had told her a sad story about Cora, but that didn't mean that would happen to her. Today, Julie started her new life as a witch. Instead of grumbling, her tummy gave off nervous flips of happiness.

After her mother braided Julie's hair, they set out together to Emerald's house. Julie's mother wanted to meet Emerald before Julie trained with her. Julie grabbed her mother's hand and skipped along the road. They sang a happy song and two passing blue jays sounded as if they chirped along with their tune.

When they arrived to Emerald's alley, Julie held her mother's hand as the wind welcomed them with a rush of air swooping around them. Julie's mother gasped as the wind pushed, then lifted them to Emerald's door. They landed against the door with a thump, their arms and legs tangled together. They giggled as they tried to straighten their hair from the windy ride. Julie wondered if the wind would ever stop trying to carry her and just trust she would go there on her own. She thought about saying something politely to the wind, but her mother interrupted her thoughts.

"Julie…?" Her mother didn't finish but waved her hand at Madam Doorika. The door blinked with red, green, and yellow lights. If a door could dance, it would look like Madam Doorika. "What in the world?" Her mother said with eyes wide, trying not to laugh.

"Mama, I forgot to tell you about Madam Doorika. Don't laugh at her. She's just glad to see us. Madam Doorika, this is my Mama. Her name is

Adelaine. Mama, this is Madam Doorika." Julie could tell her mother felt very silly introducing herself to a door, but she had the best manners of anyone Julie had ever met, so she curtsied as if Madam Doorika was a queen.

"Pleased to meet you," she said.

Madam Doorika turned a bright red like she blushed. Julie looked around for the door knocker and didn't see it. "Madam Doorika, could you please let us in?" Madam Doorika opened with a loud creak and a gold bell appeared, tinkling to announce their arrival.

Emerald's voice reached them from somewhere inside the house, "Come in. Come in. I'm in the middle of a recipe. Find me in the kitchen."

Julie took her mother's hand and they walked through the door. Madam Doorika whipped closed with such a big bang, both Julie and her mother jumped. Adelaine reached back and tried to open Madam Doorika again, but the doorknob refused to turn.

"I guess we have no choice but to stay," Adelaine said. She took a deep breath and led her daughter into the house.

CHAPTER 7

The first room they walked into held nothing more than a bench, an umbrella, a broom and some very pointy black boots. Julie wondered if she now had to wear pointy boots. After all, didn't all witches wear pointy shoes? She didn't think they looked very comfortable, but she would like some new shoes. Even on sunny days, she felt a chill swirl through the holes by her toes.

The next room looked like a living room with a big comfortable chair, a nice fire and the two cats she had seen yesterday sitting on pillows next to the fire. The white cat had blue eyes and the black cat stared at them with yellow eyes. Both of them had the fluffiest fur Julie had ever seen on a cat. Julie had just started to say hello when her mother let out a giant sneeze. Adelaine was very, very allergic to cats.

"Oh dear Ice," said the black cat in a voice like a king. "I do believe this nice woman is allergic to us."

Adelaine yelped mid sneeze. Julie's mouth plopped open and she stood frozen in place. She gulped and tried to think of something to say to a talking cat, but all she could think of was "meow" and that didn't seem all that appropriate.

"Lord Ink, look what you've done," purred the white cat. "You've scared our guests. Ink, please do apologize."

The black cat put his nose in the air. "To a human? I would never say sorry to a human, even if one of them is a witch. A human should say sorry to me for not telling me how handsome I am from the moment we met." The black cat sniffed loudly and then licked his paws.

Julie was a guest in this house and thought Ink should act more polite. But just as Julie put her hands on her hips to tell Ink to mind his manners, the white cat rolled her eyes. "I'm sorry for my friend. My name is Lady Ice and this is Lord Ink."

Adelaine sneezed a "pleased to meet you" with a curtsey. Julie curtsied too.

Julie wanted to ask these cats how they learned to talk, but then they heard Emerald from the room next to them call out, "Keep coming back, I'm in here."

Lady Ice padded over and rubbed her back against Julie's legs. "Don't worry about Ink," purred Lady Ice. "He's a grump, but harmless."

Julie smiled and squeezed her mother's hand as they pushed past a swinging red door. Adelaine stopped sneezing the moment she smelled the rosemary hanging from the ceiling. The room looked like a kitchen with a big log fire in the middle. On top of that fire sat a huge black pot bubbling with what looked like green slime, but smelled like honey.

Emerald wore bright blue gloves up to her elbows and stood with her hands deep inside the pot.

"I'm just in the middle of something," Emerald huffed distracted. She pushed a wisp of hair out of her face with her arm and then dug her arms deeper into the pot. "Ahh, there it is! Come on now," she mumbled as she pushed around in the slime. Then suddenly she pulled out a large egg. She let the slime around the egg drip back in, then used a bright orange towel to dry it off. Once clean, she carefully handed it to Julie.

Julie took the egg and held it like a baby in her arms. It felt heavy. The delicate shell was painted with swirling yellow and purple shining stars on the outside.

"It's beautiful," Julie whispered and Adelaine reached over to feel the patterns on the shell. "What is it?" Julie refused to take her eyes off it. She felt as if invisible ties bound it to her heart.

"Julie, it's yours," Emerald said smiling. "I'm not sure exactly what's inside. Only after you are a full witch will the egg hatch and reveal your Symbia."

"Symbia?" Adelaine asked. "What's a Symbia?" Julie felt too shy to ask what that big word meant.

"A Symbia is a witch's pet." Emerald explained.

"A pet?" Adelaine lifted her eyebrows. "We barely have enough food to feed our children. We can't afford to feed a pet."

Julie clutched tighter to her egg. She already loved it and didn't want to let it go.

"Oh this pet isn't something you feed," Emerald said as she sat down on a stool and took off her gloves. "Most Symbias love sweets, but they don't need human food to live. Instead, it will help make Julie a stronger witch."

Julie leaned down and whispered to the egg, "I love you already."

"Haven't you ever seen Cora's Symbia?" Emerald asked. "She has a glorious horse with silver streaks through its mane. It is her friend, but it also makes her stronger." Emerald stood back from the pot and for a moment, an image of a galloping white horse with a moon colored mane appeared right above the bubbling slime. Emerald snapped her fingers and the smoke picture drifted off in a cloud.

Adelaine nodded. "Yes, I lived with Moonbeam for many years. Cora never told me Moonbeam helped her. She just told me Moonbeam was a magic horse and she loved Moonbeam like a mother loves her child."

"Well, Julie will need her Symbia just like she needs her breath. It will make her magic stronger. Right now, the egg is getting to know Julie to figure out what she needs most. When it figures it out, it will hatch. Her Symbia creates itself as Julie's magic grows." Julie stared down at the egg and her smile sparkled. She couldn't wait to meet the creature inside. "A witch needs her Symbia just like her Symbia needs her. The two cats you met, Lady Ice and Lord Ink, are my Symbias. I was very lucky to have two born together in the same egg. They keep each other company and both have different gifts for me. Ink can be quite rude sometimes, but he gives me the power to stand up for myself. Ice gives me the power of patience. Once your Symbia is born, you will realize you could never imagine life without it."

Adelaine wrapped her arm around Julie. "Julie, it sounds like you will be a mother to this creature," Adelaine said. "I can't imagine my life without you. This Symbia will be a lot of responsibility."

Emerald nodded. "Julie, you must protect this egg with your life. If it breaks, you cannot get another one."

Julie chewed the inside of her cheek feeling overwhelmed. "But how do I take care of it? How long will it take to hatch?" Julie felt afraid she'd break it or her brothers would step on it as they wrestled around the house.

"The time for the egg to hatch is really up to you and your magic," Emerald said. "No one can ever predict when it will happen. To keep it safe, you should keep the egg with you at all times and only set it down where you know it can't get hurt."

Emerald shook her cane and a bag appeared. The bag held the softest, silkiest egg sized pillow inside. Julie put the strap over her shoulder and placed the egg carefully in the bag. The pillow wrapped itself around the egg and hugged it, just as Julie's arms had done.

"This bag will help you carry your Symbia. But Julie, you must beware of anything that will hurt it. If you ever lose your Symbia, you lose it forever. There is a terrible Wizard who lost his Symbia as a young child. He is now wicked because the good in him died with his Symbia. He is so unhappy, he cannot stand to see anyone else happy." Emerald shuttered. "You must protect your egg with your life. If you lose your Symbia, you will wish you were dead because it will hurt that much."

Adelaine patted Julie's back and whispered, "Then we will keep it safe."

Emerald clapped her hands and shook her cane. A feast magically appeared on the table next to them with meats, cheeses, breads and dainty strawberry cakes with white frosting.

"Now, let's sit down and get to know each other," Emerald said as she held out a cake for Julie.

Julie took the delicate cake and pulled up a chair to the table. When Emerald gave her a little nod, Julie began to devour her food.

For the rest of the day, Julie and Adelaine learned all about Emerald and they learned to love her. Adelaine began to trust that Emerald had Julie's best interests in mind and didn't want Julie to run off to fight the Darkness.

As they ate, Julie patted her tummy feeling so very lucky to eat such a grand meal. After lunch, Julie used her sweetest voice to ask if she could bring some food to the rest of her family. With a wave of Emerald's cane, a box appeared. The leftovers flipped in, the box snapped shut, and a ribbon tied itself around it.

"For your family," Emerald said and handed the box to Adelaine.

'Thank you, thank you, thank you," Julie sputtered. "My brothers will love it."

"Yes Emerald, thank you," Adelaine said as they stepped out the door.

'You're very welcome," Emerald said. Then she reached out to touch Julie's shoulder. "Julie, a young witch must concentrate on just her magic and not worry about how her family will eat. I can see you love your family very much. I can see your love makes your magic very strong. But love is one thing, worry is another. While your love will help you, worry will break you down. Tomorrow we will make sure you lose a bit of that worry. Tomorrow, we will teach you how to cook with your magic."

Julie nodded and gave Emerald a shy smile. But inside, Julie felt the tiniest bit of hope start to glow within her. She'd forgotten how very lovely hope felt. She gave Emerald a hug and thanked her again for the food.

As they set off to home, Julie skipped alongside her mother. Every once in awhile, she reached down and patted her egg and whispered, "I love you," just in case it could hear her.

CHAPTER 8

As soon as they got home, Julie's mother sent the boys out to collect the softest things they could find to make a bed. She didn't explain exactly why, but the older boys sprinted outside and quickly came back in with their arms full of leaves and soft grass. Benjamin, the baby, came in carrying a couple of rocks and a worm. Once they saw the box filled with food, they promptly dropped it all on the floor.

They jumped up and down and Sam hugged Julie so hard she couldn't breathe.

"Look… out… egg," she said pointing to her bag. She pulled the egg out and explained how it was the family's job to keep the egg safe. She let each boy take a turn touching it, then she used her grown up voice to order them to never hold it without her permission. When Julie turned to Benjamin, he asked if he could bite it and tried to put it in his mouth. Julie shook her head and asked him to promise to never to eat it. Benjamin stomped his foot and pouted his bottom lip, but eventually he promised.

Then they called Julie's papa into the room and sat down to the table for dinner.

After they served the food, Adelaine cleared her throat. "I have something very important to tell you," she said squeezing Julie's hand. "I'm not quite sure how to say this." She took a deep breath preparing for her sons to run out of the room screaming. "Julie is a witch."

Sam popped a cake into his mouth, then tried to look serious as he gulped down the humungous bite he'd just taken. He grinned when he finally swallowed. "Yum," he said.

Adelaine waited for them to start crying or asking more questions. Instead, Benjamin yelled out "Hurray!" then he shoved a block of cheese into his mouth just at the spot between his cheek and his teeth.

"Aren't you afraid?" Adelaine asked.

"No," Sam said with a mouthful of bread. "If we eat like this every day, Julie can be the meanest, wickedest witch around and I wouldn't care."

Jacob nodded. "We'd love her even if she couldn't feed us this way," he said. "But we always knew Julie was special. I'm not surprised." The other boys grunted in agreement between bites. Jacob shrugged and continued gobbling down his sandwich.

Julie's papa reached over to hold Julie's hand and said, "Julie, as long as you are happy, we are happy."

Julie felt like sunshine shimmered from within her. For the first time in a long time, she was happy. Just knowing her family had enough to eat untied the ball of worry that had burrowed into her chest.

That night at bedtime, Julie set the egg into its nest of grass and leaves she'd made in the box and pulled it close to her spot on the floor.

As her brothers slept around her, Julie whispered to the egg. "I guess I should tell you about my life." Julie paused, feeling silly that she was talking to an egg. Then she saw it quiver just for a second and so she continued on. "You should know I love flowers. I never pick them because I don't want to hurt them, but sometimes I would like a big beautiful flower in this room. You should know I love my brothers, but sometimes they drive me crazy. Once my brother Sam put worms in my hair because he thought it was funny. Mama made him pick them out one by one and find a safe spot for the worms back in the garden. I am pretty much afraid of the dark and sometimes afraid of lightning. I have learned some adults are nice and some are mean. I wish I had a bed and a very warm blanket. Most of all, I wish my family was safe all the time and they didn't need me to help take care of them…." On and on she went until she could barely keep her eyes open. When she finally leaned down to kiss the egg good night, she thought she heard a tiny little growl coming from it. She fell asleep with one arm in the box.

CHAPTER 9

The next day after a breakfast of leftovers, Julie skipped by herself to Emerald's alley. When she got close enough, the wind picked her up and carried her to Madam Doorika. It felt like she rode on a big cloud pillow. This time it didn't drop her, but set her down with a sigh. Madam Doorika welcomed Julie with a little song from her bell. Julie walked in with one arm in her Symbia bag protecting her precious egg.

"Good morning love," Emerald called when she saw Julie walk into the kitchen. "Today, I'd like to talk to you about spells."

With a wave of her cane, Emerald made a safe nest on the floor. "While we work, the cats will guard your Symbia." Emerald opened the swinging door from the kitchen and called out. "Ink, Ice, come here. Please do us a favor by watching over this lovely egg."

Slowly Ink and Ice slunk into the kitchen. Ink saw Julie and pushed his nose into the air with pursed lips. Julie wasn't sure if Ink was upset or if he looked that way all the time.

He sniffed. "I don't help humans, but I have nothing better to do at the moment so I guess I can help your Symbia," he said in his grand voice. He looked bored, but then snuggled up against the egg.

Ice wove around Julie's feet, rubbing up against her legs purring, "I would be happy to watch your egg, Little Witch. Please ignore Ink. He's in a bad mood this morning because he wants ice cream for breakfast."

Emerald rolled her eyes. "And I said no ice cream until he ate a healthy breakfast."

Ink made his best pouty face. "Emerald, how am I supposed to enjoy life if you don't indulge my wishes?" Ink then turned his head away and set about cleaning his paws.

Emerald sat down on a stool and Julie sat next to her.

"Ignore him," Emerald said. "I hope your Symbia isn't quite as moody as Lord Ink." Julie didn't say it out loud, but she hoped that too. "Now today you will learn how to make spells."

"Oh yay!" Julie said. "Please make your spell book appear. Where is it?" Julie looked around the kitchen thinking Emerald would shake her cane and the book would drop from the ceiling or jump out of the sink.

Emerald didn't move. "Oh that's right. You really don't know all that much about witches." Emerald winked her blue eye. "We must start from the beginning. There's no such thing as spell books. Every witch has her own spells that she makes from her mind."

Ignoring Emerald, Ink purred under Julie's feet. "Would you pretty, pretty, please get me ice cream for breakfast? Plleeeaaaaasssssssseeeeeee."

Julie leaned down to pat his head. "Sorry Ink, you have to eat a good breakfast before you have sweets."

"Fine," Ink sniffed and batted her leg with his paw. He slumped back down next to her Symbia egg. "I'm sure whatever is inside this thing is going to want me to have ice cream."

Julie couldn't help herself, she burst out laughing. Ink was a grump, but she saw the way he snuggled up against her Symbia. Under all that pompous fur, he had a heart. He just didn't like showing it.

"I suppose I do spoil him," Emerald mumbled looking sheepish as she waved her cane and two dishes of what looked like fish appeared in front of the cats. Even Ink couldn't resist whatever lay in the dish and he started eating. "But spoiling him makes me happy until he starts acting so naughty." She leaned down and patted Ink. He pressed his face against her hand and purred. "Where were we? Ahh yes, my great great great Aunt Sapphire lived a long time ago. She was the first witch to start a rumor about spell books."

Emerald wiggled her fingers and an image of a red haired witch wearing black pointy boots and an orange dress appeared.

"She even has a black hat," Julie said trying her best to show she was paying attention. Julie reached out to touch the smoky image, but it drifted off and disappeared.

Emerald nodded. "My Aunt Sapphire lived long ago in a kingdom with a powerful king. He heard about her powers and asked her to come to his castle to cast a spell to make it rain for the farmers. It hadn't rained there in a very long time and he needed Sapphire's spell to help the farmers grow food. Sapphire did as he asked and that night it rained like never before. The king promised Sapphire he would never ask for her help again, but he did. At first he asked for important spells, but then the king got greedy. He started ordering her to do spells for things he could do himself like—"

"I love this part," interrupted Ice as she cleaned her paws. "He ordered her to make a spell to tie his shoe whenever it came untied. He even ordered her to make a spell so he never had to brush his hair."

Julie giggled at the thought of such a spoiled king.

"That's right," nodded Emerald. "Lots of people actually needed her help and it wasn't a good use of her time. Many witches have special powers. Some are warriors, some are life giving witches, I am a teacher and Aunt Sapphire was a healer. One day, the king's knights came to Sapphire's house just as she helped a very sick baby. The knights ordered her to come to the castle right away. The knights said the king was about to host a grand ball with a very pretty princess and he wanted Sapphire to make the princess fall in love with him."

"When Sapphire said no and tried to stay with the baby, the knights grabbed her and threw her in the castle's dungeon," said Ice. "The king told her he would never let her out unless she swore to make spells only for him."

Emerald nodded. "Sapphire didn't want to do silly spells forever because she wanted to help people that really needed her," she said. "So Sapphire looked the king right in the eye and said she could never do magic for him because someone had stolen her book of magic spells. For years, the king sent scavengers across the land looking for that book. Of course, he never found it and he left Sapphire alone because he thought she'd lost her magical powers. Ever since, witches everywhere use that excuse to avoid magic when they don't feel a spell is the right thing to do."

Julie rested her chin in her hands, feeling suddenly overwhelmed. "How will I know when a spell is the right thing to do?"

"You follow your heart and ask yourself if you feel right about it. If you listen, your magic will tell you."

"Okay," Julie said slowly, "but how do I make magic without a spell book then?"

"Your spells start in your mind and then burst to the world from within you."

Julie just shook her head imagining stardust and rainbows shooting out of her ears. She didn't think that sounded very comfortable. "What? I have spells just swirling around in my body?"

"Well, not exactly. Spells aren't things, they are your thoughts. Witches make spells by using their imagination. Your imagination is the greatest spell maker in the world. Watch." Emerald shook her cane and two tea cups with tea and little sandwiches appeared. A napkin flew out of a drawer, looked at Julie with little napkin eyes and landed on Julie's lap. "When you want to do a spell, you imagine what it would feel like when it is done. Making spells starts with your imagination first, then the magic flows from there."

Julie took a bite of a sandwich and a crumb fell onto the napkin.

"Yummy yum yum," gobbled the napkin as it made a mouth shape and ate the crumb. Julie froze, feeling unsure of what to do. She gave a nervous smile and continued to eat her sandwich. When she swallowed her last bite, the napkin jumped up off her lap and ate the crumbs on her plate saying, "Gobble, gobble, gobble" and then flopped back onto Julie's lap.

"Did my imagination make that napkin just talk to me?" Julie said sitting very still in case the napkin was still hungry and tried to bite her finger next.

Emerald laughed, "No, that was my spell. I wanted a napkin to appear, but sometimes magic has a mind of its own and gives us what it thinks we want."

Emerald shook her cane again and the napkin made a mouth shape to say, "Goodbye Little Witch," and flew right back into the drawer.

Julie's brow furrowed. "I don't understand. My mama has always said I have a big imagination, but no matter how much I imagine, nothing magical has ever happened."

"Well, every witch needs something to help her bring the magic out," said Emerald. "It's called a conductor. Some witches use magic wands. I use my cane. We have to find a conductor for you." Emerald shook her cane and made a mirror appear in front of Julie.

Julie sighed when she saw herself. She wore her tired grey dress, saggy socks and sad, holey shoes. She didn't have a conductor and started to look around the kitchen to maybe use a spatula as a wand. Then her sparkling necklace caught her eye.

"Can I use Cora's necklace?" Julie asked as she put one hand on the shells. The necklace let off a spark. Julie flinched and pulled her hand away.

"Yes. Cora meant for you to have it. In your life, you will have many different conductors, but this necklace will be your first." Julie touched the necklace again. It let out a burst like a firecracker and a puff of purple smoke.

"What's something you want more than anything in the world?" Emerald asked, but she already knew.

Julie didn't need any time to think about it. "I wish my brothers, my mama and papa never went to bed hungry." Julie whispered it and then looked at her saggy socks. She thought it was too much to ask for her tummy to be full too.

"What about you Julie?" Emerald touched Julie's chin and made Julie look at her. "Don't you think you deserve that too?"

Julie looked into Emerald's eyes and felt the tears sliding down her cheeks. "I would like food too," she said and gulped. She reached up to wipe the tears from her cheek. One turned silver, rolled off the back of her hand, and floated into her pocket.

"Then make it so." Emerald said softly, letting go of Julie's chin. Julie closed her eyes and felt humming from her necklace against her neck. She reached up and touched it and heard popping sparks. Wind somehow picked up and twisted and then twirled around Julie like a tornado. The table rattled and the dishes clanged in the cabinet. The walls shook. Ink and Ice moved closer to Julie's egg and put their little paws over it to keep it safe.

The noise was so loud, Emerald had to yell. "Imagine a place in your house where you will always have food. Not so much food you waste it, but just enough to feed your family. Where is that place, Julie? What do you see?"

Julie kept one hand on the necklace and the other she raised in the air. She imagined her little house. "The pantry in my kitchen. It has a door, and I see my mama opening that door and finding dinner there every night. I see her smiling, my brothers happy, and my papa pats his full tummy."

"Julie, do you see yourself there too?" The wind got louder and the cabinet doors banged open and shut. The napkin peeked its head out of the drawer, shivered and hid back inside. The table blew from one end of the kitchen to the other. Still, Julie was lost in her thoughts and didn't notice any of it.

At first, Julie couldn't imagine herself there in her kitchen, but then she saw herself sitting at her table with a full plate of food. In her mind, she picked up a fork and took a bite of mashed potatoes and gravy. She tasted the salt from the gravy and the mashed potatoes squished in her mouth. Just when she imagined she swallowed that bite, a loud red spark burst like a firework from her necklace. Julie opened her eyes and the wind stopped.

"It is done," Emerald said. "We'll work on controlling that magic tomorrow. Now run home and see the gift you made for you and your family." Emerald gave Julie a big hug and helped Julie gently put her egg back into her bag. Just as Julie turned to leave, Emerald leaned down and stared into Julie's eyes, "Julie, your Aunt Cora was right. You are the greatest witch I have ever seen."

CHAPTER 10

Julie walked into her door expecting the smell of dinner on the table. Instead, she stepped into her quiet little kitchen and watched as her mother stirred porridge on the stove. Her brothers wrestled on the floor.

"Mama, I thought we were going to have mashed potatoes for dinner," Julie said giving her mama a big hug. She started to cry as she told her mother about her day. "Emerald lied. I didn't make magic for us. There's no food." The boys stopped fighting and sat still watching Julie.

Sam got up and hugged her. "You already made magic for us by bringing us dinner last night Julie. You don't have to do it every night."

Adelaine put her spoon down. "Wait, let's think about this," she said and walked around the kitchen. "You saw our pantry? This cabinet?"

She pointed to the big cabinet door next to the stove. Normally, the cabinet sat empty because they never had any food to put in it. Julie couldn't remember the last time they'd even opened it. Adelaine put her hand on the cabinet door, and without much thought, swung it open. As soon as she did, mashed potatoes flew out, splattering her in the face and covering her whole head. She closed the cabinet door with a bang.

"What... How?" Adelaine sputtered. She looked like someone had just dipped her face and head into snow. She had to wipe the mashed potatoes from her eyelids before she could even open her eyes.

They all sat very quiet for a moment and then Julie couldn't help it. She started to laugh. Not just a little giggle, but big belly laughs. Hearing Julie, the boys started too and Sam rolled on the floor holding his belly as he roared with laughter. Adelaine tried to look mad with her hands on her hips, but couldn't hide it any longer and burst out laughing too.

Then Benjamin started crying and reaching for the cabinet because he wanted mashed potatoes to splat on his head too. "It's not fair that Mama is the only one who gets mashed potatoes in her hair," he pouted.

Adelaine used a towel to clean herself off and then mopped up the potatoes on the floor. "You are right Benny. It isn't fair."

Just then Julie's papa came home after a long day looking for a job. He gave everyone big hugs and slumped down at the table.

He sighed. "No work today. I'm so very sorry."

Adelaine winked at her kids and said very sweetly, "Welcome home Jack, I'm sure you will find work soon. Would you mind getting a cup out of that cabinet for me?" She pointed to the mashed potato cabinet.

Julie's papa had such a very horrible day looking for work that he didn't even stop to think they didn't keep the cups in that cabinet. He was always helpful in the kitchen and so he stood up and walked over to the cabinet.

"I'm sorry family that I didn't find work today. Tomorrow will be another—" Julie's papa looked at his family as he talked so he wasn't even looking at the cabinet when he opened it very wide. As soon as he did, it was like a big fire hose of mashed potatoes sprayed out covering him from head to toe. He looked like a mashed potato snowman. He was so surprised that he just stood there with his mouth open as the mashed potatoes exploded out of the cabinet, spraying all over and filling his mouth. Finally, he realized he should close the cabinet and slammed it shut with a bang.

"Julie, what have you done?" He said trying to hide his smile as he shook mashed potatoes from his ears. The kids laughed so hard they couldn't breathe. Adelaine leaned over giggling and trying to catch her breath. Julie's papa ran over to Julie and gave her a big hug covering her with mashed potatoes too.

That night the family took turns trying to figure out how to get mashed potatoes into a bowl for dinner. The cabinet kept exploding more and more mashed potatoes as they opened the door again and again. The mashed potatoes covered the kitchen from top to bottom and the baby rolled around trying to make a mashed potato cave. Benjamin put some extra mashed potatoes in his hair so he'd look just like his mama. Finally, Sam opened the door just a crack while Julie held a bowl to catch them. They cleaned the kitchen together and with mashed potatoes in their hair, they sat down for dinner. The mashed potatoes were the most delicious potatoes anyone had ever tasted. Julie let them melt in her mouth as she smiled at her happy family.

As they finished dinner, Adelaine said, "Thank you Julie for that wonderful meal. But tonight is now bath night." The boys groaned. "And tomorrow, Julie would you pretty please ask Emerald how to turn down your mashed potatoes faucet just a bit?" Adelaine winked at her daughter and the family roared with laughter.

CHAPTER 11

The days passed quickly. In the mornings, Julie woke up in her new comfy bed she had made with her magic and watched her sleeping brothers in their beds snoozing under their big warm blankets. As Julie opened her eyes, her fingers would tingle, and her toes would twitch as her magic woke up too. Her bed had a special spot for her egg on its own pillow next to her head. She would start chattering to her egg as soon as she woke up. Sometimes, her Symbia would hum, growl or let out a little meep as a good morning.

Emerald trained with Julie every day. At first, Emerald just helped Julie understand her magic. Their first task was to help Julie's magic cabinet behave. The next night after the mashed potatoes explosion, Julie didn't quite trust her magic even after Emerald helped her. So Julie told her mama to put a bowl on her head like a helmet and open the door slowly. Julie's mama inched open the cabinet and squeezed her eyes shut just in case something flew out. No mashed potatoes sprayed her head, so she opened her eyes. There, she found a beautiful turkey dinner, with peas and sweet corn sitting on a big silver platter. The family cheered from their hiding spots behind the table and then sat down ready to eat.

Adelaine pulled out the platter, but didn't worry about closing the door. She'd accidentally left a sweet blueberry pie behind, so it whizzed out and almost hit Sam in the head as it plopped down next to Benjamin. Before Adelaine could stop him, Benjamin put both hands right into that pie, scooping out handfuls and putting pie in his pockets for later.

From that day forward, whenever they were hungry, they just opened the cabinet and found just enough food for their family, but never too much. As the days went by, Julie's family started to forget how it felt to have a grumbling in their tummies and Julie liked the feeling of losing some of her worry in her heart.

Things Julie learned those first few weeks:

1. Her magic wasn't always perfect. She had to tell it exactly what she wanted or it would guess.

Once she imagined pillows for her bed, but she made cloud pillows instead. She thought they looked very comfortable, but when she rested her head on them they felt wet and a bit stormy. She had to stay up late trying to make real pillows while her brothers kept complaining the thunder booms from the clouds kept them awake.

She also learned this lesson when she made warm clothes for her family. Julie made a sensible green dress, a little ribbon for her hair, and fast shoes for herself. She looked at herself in the mirror and twirled and twirled, so happy to wear a little color. She took the tears she had saved in her pocket and put them in her new dress. She didn't know why, but it seemed a sensible thing to do. Her new dress fit perfectly, but when she looked at her brother Sam, his shirt and trousers looked a bit big. So she put in her mind she wanted them to shrink, but her magic got mixed up. When she opened her eyes, she had accidentally shrunk Sam into a tiny person the size of her finger. Julie scooped him up and ran as fast as she could to Emerald's house for help.

All the while, Sam squeaked at her. "You better get me big again Julie! I will never forgive you if I'm tiny all my life!"

Once Emerald helped her turn him back to his proper size, Sam was so relieved he just hugged Julie and made her promise she would never shrink him again. She did her best to keep that promise, but her magic was still a little shaky. She did accidentally shrink him again one more time, but just for a minute and she fixed it right away. Sam was pretty mad at her and just squeaked, "Julie you promised!" in a tiny voice before she got him big again. Julie said she was sorry, but thought it was really his fault for jumping in the way of a spell just as she tried to make Benjamin a new toy soldier. She decided not to argue about it when he pulled her into a big hug to thank her for returning him back to normal.

2. Her magic did not let her be greedy.

Julie wanted to make sure she never had to worry about her family's money again. So she tried to use her magic to make a huge treasure chest of gold and jewels. But when she opened the treasure chest, she only found a small bag with a sensible amount of money to take care of her family. When the bag ran out, it filled itself again. Julie realized her magic wouldn't make her family really rich, but she decided that was okay. She'd much prefer the happiness her family felt since finding her magic, over any jewels in a treasure chest. Julie decided that as long as her family had enough, she didn't need more.

3. Her magic didn't let her be mean.

Julie was a very good girl and she tried to be nice all the time, but she was a little girl after all and being a little girl sometimes meant she made mistakes. When she had her food, warm clothes and a soft bed, she got to thinking about those awfully mean adults she met when she was looking for a job. She thought about that mean baker and how he had spat food out of his mouth yelling at her to go away. She decided she wanted to teach him a lesson. So one day, she marched into that bakery through the front door and walked right up to his counter.

The baker had a big mixing bowl of flour next to him. He clearly did not recognize her because he said in a very sweet voice, "Hello lovely girl. What can I sell you today?"

Julie stood there with her hands on her hips. "I'm the little girl that came to your back door to ask for help. You were very mean and I'm here to teach you a lesson."

His brow furrowed for a moment, but then his mouth fell open and his eyes bulged when he remembered her. He couldn't understand how that sad hungry girl now looked so happy wearing a pretty green dress with a ribbon in her hair. She touched her necklace and imagined the baker's flour dumping all over his head. But nothing happened. Her magic felt locked inside her chest and refused to come out. She pressed her magic again and still nothing happened.

The baker towered over her with his hands leaning on the counter. "What exactly are you going to do child?" he sneered as his face pinched into a cruel smile.

Watching that nasty look spread across his doughy face somehow unlocked Julie's magic. She felt a swirl around her chest and her magic danced out to the baker. Without understanding what her magic was doing, a blue cloud of sparkles covered him and floated into his ears, his mouth, and even his nose. Just as the cloud disappeared, a sign appeared on the baker's door that said, "Free bread for all hungry children."

The baker ground his teeth when he saw it and stomped over to pull it off, but he couldn't. He grimaced and grunted as he tried to push, scrape and tear at it. When that didn't work, he slammed his body against it. Still nothing happened. He reached over and grabbed a hammer sitting by his counter. He whacked it into the sign over and over again. Sweat dripped from the baker's bald head and his face turned an angry shade of purple as he pounded at the sign. Still, Julie's magic stood strong and the sign stayed.

The baker stomped back over to his counter and shook the hammer at Julie. "GET... OUT... OF... HERE!" He screamed through clenched teeth, but just then a dirty girl about Julie's age came into the bakery.

"Sir, can I please have some bread?" the girl mumbled pointing to the sign. "I'm very hungry."

Julie glanced at the furious baker and thought about running, but then she saw the girl's sunken cheeks and hungry eyes. Julie wondered if she had looked that hungry, but once she heard the girl's grumbling tummy she knew she had.

The baker's eyes oozed hate at Julie. He scrunched up his face trying to say no. But instead, out popped, "Of course, you can have as much as you need."

The baker slapped his hands over his mouth trying to keep it from saying more. Then he grabbed a hold of the counter and tried to keep himself from walking over to his bread. But his legs went the other way and finally his fingers scraped the counter leaving long marks in the wood as they slid off. The baker strained to hold his arms to his side, but one arm picked up two loaves of bread and handed them to the little girl.

"Thank you Sir," the girl said as she started to cry tears of happiness. The baker would never admit it, but a tiny part of his heart glowed just a bit because he had helped the little girl. But a little bit of glowing wouldn't change his heart right away. Julie saw it would take a lot of little children eating a lot of bread to make that man a very nice person. She touched her necklace and sent a quick spell to the baker's basket to refill whenever he gave a loaf of bread to a hungry child. She hoped that if he gave away enough bread, he might become nice one day.

Julie curtsied to the baker and then followed the little girl out the door. She heard the baker cussing behind her as the door slid shut. After they walked a safe distance away from the bakery, Julie touched her necklace and a little red velvet coin purse appeared in her hand. Inside, it held a few coins. Julie tried to hand it to the girl, but the girl just stared at Julie as she clutched the bread to her chest.

"My name is Olive," the girl said with suspicious eyes. She nodded at the purse. "What's that?"

Julie leaned over to whisper so only Olive could hear. "This bag holds good magic. You can have it. Just don't be greedy and it will refill whenever you need it." Julie held the bag out for her.

Olive reached out and let her fingers slide along the velvet, but still she didn't take it. "You don't want nothin' from me?"

"No," Julie shook her head. "I was hungry once and I will never forget how that felt. I want to help. Take it. It's yours."

Olive blinked, then snatched the purse out of Julie's hand. "Thank you for your kindness," Olive mumbled as she turned and sprinted into a dark alley. She never even looked back. Julie stood there for a moment and felt the curious sensation of her magic buzzing under her fingernails as it grew stronger.

Julie turned and walked straight to Emerald's house. She found Emerald in the kitchen cooking over her black cauldron filled with boiling brown sludge. Julie wrapped her arms around Emerald and let the story tumble out. Julie didn't want to admit that she had tried to dump flour on the baker, but she wanted to know why her magic hadn't listened to her.

Emerald pointed to a chair at the table. "Sit Julie," she said looking worried. "You made a mistake today and it's not something I can fix."

Julie sank down into the chair and twisted the sleeve of her dress trying to avoid Emerald's gaze.

Emerald sighed. "Your magic tried to stop you, but you pushed on. Your magic is yours, but it tried to teach you how to use it with kindness."

Emerald shook her cane and a scroll jumped out of the brown slime in the pot. It plopped down in front of Julie and splattered her just a bit. Julie shook off the slime and unrolled it. It read:

Julie's Rules of Magic

Always use magic for good. Never use it to hurt. If you try to use your magic for bad, it won't listen unless you seek the Darkness. Never seek the Darkness!

Never be greedy. A spell should give just enough, and not too much.

Be careful who sees your magic. Strangers might not understand. Friends could ask you to do things you don't want to do. Witches and Wizards can be jealous. There will always be someone who wants your magic. Choose wisely with whom you share your gifts.

A witch cannot make spells to bring back the dead, time travel, or live forever.

A witch's love makes her magic stronger.

Emerald gave Julie a hug. "The most important lesson of all is to show love and love will feed your magic. But today, you made a terrible mistake by showing off your magic."

Julie chewed on her bottom lip feeling worried. She thought about Olive eating bread and holding her new coin purse. Julie's magic pulsed under her skin and stirred that happy feeling with her guilt.

Julie stared down at her feet. "I'm… I'm sorry, but that little girl needed my help. I promise I'll be more careful."

"You have to be," warned Emerald. "A witch should never be as obvious as you were today. I'm worried you shared your gifts with the wrong people. You can't help everyone. You must learn how to decide who deserves to see your magic."

Julie nodded and tried to forget that maybe Olive wasn't the right person to help. Julie started to feel scared and tears pricked her eyes.

Emerald patted Julie's head. "Tomorrow will be a new day, my love," she said. "You don't have to be perfect, just learn from your mistakes. That's how we become better witches."

On the walk home, Julie talked to her Symbia egg and did her best to describe Olive and how happy it had made her to help another girl.

"You should come see this world my pet. You would love all the good things here." She reached into the bag and felt the egg quiver under her fingers. But she couldn't shake the feeling that someday she'd pay for her mistake.

CHAPTER 12

Julie practiced and practiced. She learned how to make potions for love, potions for the sick, spells to help the weather, and just about any other spells she could imagine.

Julie's favorite spell was the spell to give animals a voice to talk to her. She loved to skip along the road toward Emerald's house and turn her voice into a bird song to sing for the birds to come see her. The birds would swoop down from the sky and land on her shoulder to sing about their lives. From the birds, she learned about faraway lands and beautiful places. They told her silly things too. Like how to catch a worm in her human mouth and how to make a nest out of a shoe. She learned they loved humans, but were very scared of them.

One morning as Julie stepped out of her house, a raven flapped down and landed on her shoulder.

"How are you little raven?" Julie asked, but he inched along her shoulder and just pressed his face to her cheek.

"Oh Julie," he sighed. "I need a hug."

Weeks ago, they had met and spent a lovely day playing hide and seek in the forest together, but she hadn't seen him since. She patted his head as she walked.

"Why such a sad face?" she asked.

He nuzzled against her ear. "I've just come from the most terrible place. It's at the edge of the ocean, but it felt like it's at the end of the world. An evil wizard lives in a dark castle. He burned down all the trees and scorched the flowers. I've never seen something so terrible." He shivered and then sniffed.

Julie wondered if he described where her Aunt Cora lived, but she didn't ask. He seemed too scared and she didn't want to make him more upset.

"I'm sorry to hear that," she said. She pulled him off her shoulder and cradled him in her hands. "What can I do to make it better? My brothers collected a bunch of worms and left them by the back door of the house. Would you like some? You are welcome to help yourself."

"Ahh, thank you Julie. Do you think maybe I could build a nest at your house for awhile?"

"Oh, of course," she said. She felt relieved not to talk about that scary place. Something about it sent a shiver up her spine. "I know the robins took up a spot in the oak tree and the canaries are on the roof. But I think the maple has room as long as you don't mind owls."

The raven thanked her for listening and sat on her shoulder for a bit longer until he sighed and flapped to the sky. As Julie watched him soar, she held her breath. She knew there were terrible things out in the world, but today she felt the sun shine on her face and so she shook the scary thoughts out of her head. She'd pushed the thoughts so far out of her mind, she forgot to even ask Emerald about the scary land when she reached her house.

CHAPTER 13

On one particularly lovely day, Emerald met Julie at Madam Doorika with a broom in her hand.

"Good morning," she said waving at Julie. "Time for a field trip Little Witch."

The broom floated up and Emerald daintily sat down on it. Ink and Ice hopped up making themselves comfortable on the broom's straw.

"Come on," Emerald winked and held out her hand for Julie. "Hop on."

"Ugg," Julie said and sighed. "You want me on there? To fly?"

Emerald tried to stay cheery and her smile widened, ignoring Julie's bad attitude. Emerald had a knack for pretending everything was okay even when Julie was upset. At times, Julie found it completely aggravating.

"Yes, Julie," Emerald said in her sing song voice keeping a smile plastered on her face as she reached out her hand. "Today we fly. Cheers to flying!"

Julie gulped, but didn't argue. She scrambled onto the front of the broom and Emerald wrapped one arm around her. Julie still felt like she might tumble off at any second. She gripped the broom handle harder and scrunched her eyes shut.

"Ready for a lovely adventure?" Emerald asked.

"No," Julie grumbled, but Emerald just ignored her.

"Alright, I haven't flown in quite some time," Emerald muttered. "Let's see here... okay... I believe my spell word to make my broom take off is... well... hmm... okay yes... it's Pumpernickel."

Nothing happened. Emerald had explained to Julie that while witches didn't need spell books, Emerald had given certain objects their own spell word so she didn't have to conjure up the same spell every time she wanted it. Now, in Emerald's old age she started to forget all her spell words.

Ink huffed. "That's your spell word to fluff my fur! I hate Pumpernickel!"

Julie glanced back and saw Ink's fur standing straight up as if his fur had come alive. He didn't look like a cat, he looked like a fur ball with eyes.

"Oh, right," Emerald muttered. "Stop pouting. I think you look very handsome." But even Julie could see Emerald's eyes grow wider. "Dearest spells, please stop Pumpernickel," Ink bristled as his hair started to lower back down. "Please start to fly. The spell word is… La Ti Da."

The broom heard the words and lurched upwards and then bucked them around the alley almost throwing them off. Julie squeaked and gripped the broom until her knuckles turned white. When they started to spin, Julie gagged, feeling as if she might throw up.

"Oops!" Emerald said, unruffled that the broom had now started to hop up and down in the air. "Silly me, that's my spell word for when we play broom soccer with the other ladies in the witch club. Let's see here, ahh yes, the spell word to fly is…" she paused for a second biting her lip hoping she got it right, "Skippidy Dippidy Do!"

With those words, the broom stopped spinning and gently rose to the air. Everyone sighed, including the broom. Julie's stomach still churned and she tried to breathe in the fresh air to settle it.

Emerald peeked over Julie's shoulder. "Julie, I do believe you are a bit green."

"I want off," Julie grumbled. As they rose above the rooftops, she felt her panic rise with them. "Just drop me down and I'll walk." She squeezed her eyes shut and clutched the broom so tight her hands ached.

"Oh no," Emerald said. "Not an option today. Where we're going is too far to walk. Just breathe, open your eyes and enjoy the ride."

"Easy for you to say," Julie said weakly. She flickered open her eyes for just a second and glanced at the tiny houses below. The panic choked her and she closed her eyes with a snap. "Not enjoying," she mumbled and tried to concentrate on breathing to distract herself. They flew for awhile longer until Emerald floated the broom down to land in a big empty field outside of town.

When the earth touched her feet, Julie tumbled off the broom onto the ground. "I am never, ever, doing that again," she sputtered.

Emerald just stood over her without saying anything. Julie looked up and groaned.

"Oh no," Julie said. "Don't tell me flying is my lesson for today!" She flopped her head onto the grass and covered her face. "Emerald, I just can't!"

"You can do it and you will," Emerald said holding out a hand to help Julie up. Julie took it and stood up, but refused to look at her. "Little Witch, how would you keep yourself safe if you were in danger?"

Julie looked down at her small hands. They wouldn't be of much use in a fight. She shrugged. "I'd use my magic."

"How? What if a monster chased you? What would you do?"

Julie felt this wasn't a fair question because Emerald knew Julie was terrified at the thought of monsters. "I'd tell it to please leave me alone," she answered in a small voice.

"Well, what if the monster won't listen and just wants to eat you?"

Julie shivered. She didn't like Emerald's questions and thought Emerald was being mean. After all of her magic practice, Julie knew she was still not very brave. She didn't need Emerald to point it out to her.

"I'd run," Julie said, "and I'd use my magic to make me run like the wind." Julie liked this idea because she practiced this spell with her brothers and they loved it when she made them run so fast their legs churned in a blur.

"What if you were somewhere so far away, you couldn't just run for help?" Emerald asked. Julie really didn't want to think about being in a place far away from Emerald and her parents. She shifted on her feet and kicked at the dirt.

"I guess I could learn to fly," she said in a whisper, then shrugged. "But I don't have a broom."

Julie touched her necklace and closed her eyes trying to calm her racing heart. But the thought of flying must have wrapped itself around her spells, because when she opened her eyes, she saw that she floated above Emerald's head. She screamed and tried to use her arms to push herself down again, but she just flapped them in the air wildly and stayed floating. Emerald grabbed one of

Julie's shoes and yanked her down. When Julie felt her feet touch the dirt, she ordered them to stay.

Emerald shook her cane and made a nest for Julie's Symbia. Julie gently laid the egg down into it. Ink and Ice had just chased a butterfly through the grass, but they now ran over and nestled next to Julie's egg. They loved the Symbia as much as Julie did and had become very good protectors of it.

Julie took a deep breath. "Alright, let's go," she grumbled. "Should I make a broom?"

"Julie, you don't need a broom to fly," Emerald said. "I use a broom because I'm old and my aching back needs a place to sit. Some witches need a broom because they don't know how to fly without one. Your magic is so strong, you can fly without a broom." Emerald stooped down to put her hands on Julie's shoulders. "Julie, today you will learn to fly, but you also need to learn how to fight. You must learn how to protect yourself when you can't run or fly away. Today we fly. Tomorrow you fight. Understand?"

Julie didn't like the way Emerald's words sounded so scary. "Emerald, I'm not brave enough to fight," Julie said. "Can I just do a spell to make myself brave?"

✳ ✿ ✳

"I'm sorry dear, no. Bravery is not something you can make with magic. You earn your bravery when you face your fears and still go on."

"Then what is the use of having magic if I still feel afraid?" Julie kicked a rock and sent it rolling away from her. She didn't usually act this way, but being brave was important to her. It frustrated her that she couldn't just do a spell to make her scared feelings go away.

"You are a witch, but you must still live life. To really live is to understand what makes you afraid and conquer it. If you live your life afraid, you will never do all that you should, because the worst fear of all is the fear of failure."

"Why can't life just be easy all the time?" Julie sighed. "I'd like that better."

"An easy life is boring," Emerald said, waving her hand in the air as if to push the thought away. "Your easiest life would be to lie in bed all day and never walk outside. People would feed you mushy food with spoons while you just sat there. Would you like to sit all day long and never play outside?"

Julie giggled and then shook her head. "Of course not."

"Yes Little Witch, you run and you play. Sometimes you fall and get hurt, but you always get up. Bravery works the same way. If you never felt afraid, it would be because you weren't really living. You would miss out on life's greatest adventures. Bravery comes when you feel afraid, but you quiet the fear to fight for what you want. You should never let fear stop you from chasing your dreams. Julie, when you quiet your fear, you will be the greatest witch that has ever existed." Emerald whispered the last word and it swirled around Julie's head and danced next to her ears.

Julie shook her head. "I'm not sure I believe you. This fear is always with me."

"Trust me," Emerald said. "Trust in yourself. Today you will learn to trust your magic to fly. You should learn to trust your magic in everything you do. Believe in yourself and you will do great things. But you will never know unless you try."

Julie stared into Emerald's eyes and then sighed. "Okay, I'll try."

Emerald smiled. "Very good Little Witch! Now, let's hope your first time flying goes a lot smoother than mine. When I first learned, I flew right into a house, bounced off it, and landed in a pond."

"Not making me feel brave," Julie grumbled. She closed her eyes and touched her necklace, imagining her feet floating up. She felt her feet raise just inches off the ground and she shrieked. She plopped down to the ground with a thump. "I'm too scared to fly," she moaned with frustrated tears.

"Julie, trust that you can keep yourself safe. Would you like me to fly with you?" Julie nodded and Emerald shook her cane and her broom floated up to her. "I will be right here with you."

Julie clutched Emerald's hand and closed her eyes again. She imagined breathing in a cloud and let that feeling fill her lungs like a balloon. Her feet rose from the earth. As Julie floated up, Emerald whispered, "Skippidy Dippidy Do" to raise her broom with her. Julie squeezed Emerald's hand so tight she practically crushed it, but Emerald didn't complain.

When Julie finally opened her eyes, she realized they floated so high the clouds curled into their hair. Emerald sat smiling at Julie from her perch atop her broom.

"Wow," Julie whispered. "Flying feels like the wind wrapped me up in a floating cocoon. I feel like I'm swimming through the air."

"Isn't it incredible?" Emerald asked. "Breathe in the beauty and enjoy yourself."

Julie squinted into the horizon and saw where the sun rose in the morning and the earth met the sky. She'd never considered what lay beyond her town and now her stomach flipped with a dream of what lived there. The houses and trees below them now looked like tiny toys.

"It's... it's... stunning," Julie said and felt her fear unlock just a bit as delight filled the spaces her fear left behind.

Just then, a little yellow canary flew up and landed on Julie's shoulder.

"Hello," it tweeted in its little voice. "Where are your wings, Little Witch?" The bird pointed its beak at Julie's arms. "Oh, there they are. Would you like to play?"

"Um, yes," Julie said, giving herself a chance to meet a new friend.

"Follow me," the canary chirped then dove into the air. Julie spread her arms like wings. Then very slowly, let go of Emerald's hand for just a second, but grabbed it again.

"Trust in yourself," Emerald reminded her. "Believe."

Julie's throat tightened and her heart beat so fast she shook. "I believe in me," she whispered and felt her magic begin to glow from within her. As she slowly let go of Emerald's hand, she soared.

"Julie," Emerald called from behind her. "I'll go stay with your Symbia. Will you be okay to find your way back?"

Julie kept her eyes locked on the canary and whispered, "Yes, I think so." She wasn't sure if Emerald even heard her, but Emerald turned her broom and flew away.

"First time in the air?" the canary tweeted as if it was perfectly natural to see a person flying through the clouds.

Julie nodded and tried to breathe. She felt the wind dancing through her hair and the clouds hugging her. She flew higher with the canary and started to relax. She dipped and swirled in the air with a freedom she'd never felt before. She followed the little canary into a storm cloud and felt afraid again as the dark inched around her. She didn't like the dark and hated thunder. Right before she truly started to panic, the thick cloud cleared. Bursting into the light, Julie's eyes squinted in the sun.

The canary chirped at her, "Welcome to the Bird Playground, Little Witch."

As Julie's eyes adjusted to the bright sun, she saw hundreds of birds singing and playing. She looked down and realized the clouds hid this place from human eyes. She floated and giggled at the sight of all the birds together. Blue jays raced robins, with a hawk acting as a referee. Several crows danced to a beat made by an owl saying, "whoo whoo, whoo whoo." Two hawks practiced their cloud dives. Several birds grouped together as one parakeet squawked, "Get your feathers groomed. Come look pretty," and a macaw and a parakeet set about grooming a red robin's feathers.

Julie felt delighted by the joy she saw in the birds. As soon as the birds noticed her, they all chirped and sang a beautiful song welcoming her. Then the birds fluttered over in a swarm of every color imaginable to welcome her, rubbing their feathers against her cheek.

After she laughed and said, "Pleased to meet you" to all the birds that wanted to meet the flying witch, she decided it was time to fly back home.

"Thank you for your help birds," Julie said as she started to fly away. "Thank you for sharing your playground with me. I do hope we meet again."

They all chirped, tweeted, crowed and squawked their goodbyes. The little canary flew with Julie out of the cloud and then landed on Julie's hand, giving her a sweet peck with her beak.

"Have fun Little Witch," the canary chirped. "I'm going back to play."

"Thank you!" Julie called and then spread her arms wide and floated on her back. She felt the glorious sun on her face. "I did it!" Julie yelled.

As she breathed in the freedom of flying, her fear shrank and quieted. She understood now what Emerald had tried to tell her. If she had been too afraid to try, she would have never felt the wind on her cheeks or met all her new friends. Because she decided to try, she didn't just float, she soared.

CHAPTER 14

"Today, I must fight," Julie whispered and wrapped her arms around her body, giving herself a hug. She felt sick to her stomach and she couldn't push away the lump in her chest. Yesterday, she had landed back into the field, her cheeks flushed with such happiness she felt as if she might float away again at just the thought of flying.

But that was yesterday. Today, Julie arrived with Emerald to that same field and somehow the field looked uglier and meaner. The field had soft grass growing on rolling hills, but today it looked like everything wanted to hurt her. The rocks now looked sharp and the grass looked like it hid something terrible. On the outside of the field grew a forest with trees taller than houses. Today, she thought those trees looked like monsters rocking back and forth in the breeze. Yesterday she felt triumphant, now the worry burrowed deep inside her.

Julie was a sweet girl who hated fighting. Of course, she had three brothers so her house was constantly noisy with wrestling and rough play. Her brothers would use any excuse to pile on top of each other, grabbing at each other's hair, arms and legs. Someone would eventually get hurt and Julie was always the one to comfort them.

Even when she was a baby, Julie cried when she saw another baby crying. Julie had a very tender heart and tried to make sure everyone was happy all the time. To fight meant to try and hurt someone and she never wanted to hurt anyone. She didn't count when she tried to dump flour on the mean baker, she considered that trying to teach him a lesson. No, Julie didn't understand why she had to fight. Because she did not understand, she was in a foul mood.

Julie scanned the field and saw Ink and Ice jumping and running through the grass.

"They sure don't care about me today," she huffed miserably. She knew they cared about her, but she was in such a sour mood it felt okay to be mad at them for a while. Julie sent a silent wish to the world to be back in Emerald's kitchen practicing love potions. "Instead, I'm here on this dirty field having no fun," Julie mumbled, kicking the dirt in frustration. She thought about holding Emerald's hand, but instead crossed her arms over her chest.

"I don't want to fight," Julie announced. She stomped her foot and refused to look at Emerald. "I'm not going to be good at it, so why are you trying to ruin my day?"

"Julie, please do not take your fear out on me," Emerald said. "It is particularly unpleasant. I love you very much, but I wish you could see I'm only trying to make sure you stay safe."

Julie felt a little bad for her nasty behavior, but she didn't uncross her arms. "I'm sorry Emerald. I just feel horribly scared."

Emerald sighed. "Julie, you have got to learn to protect yourself. Every witch has to learn. Someone might try to steal your magic or trap you so you make magic for them." She tugged at Julie's chin to make Julie look at her. "You should know by now you can do this. As a witch, you can use your magic to protect yourself. You are only limited by your imagination."

"I won't fight. I'll just use my invisibility spell."

An invisibility spell sounded easiest. Julie could never completely transport herself magically somewhere else, but she could make herself invisible. She loved playing hide and seek with her brother Benjamin by sitting in the grass, turning herself invisible and letting Benjamin pad around the yard hunting for her.

"That may work sometimes, but no witch can just magically put herself somewhere else. Even if you are invisible, you still have to run or fly or find a way to get to a safe place."

"Humpf," Julie grumbled.

"I think you are on to a good start though," Emerald said trying to keep her voice cheery. "Start thinking about how you can use your magic to protect yourself and your magic will answer. Plus, a witch has something else amazing to protect her."

"Her witch friends?" Julie asked, crossing her fingers hoping Emerald could just protect her all the time.

"Not exactly. Your Symbia can help you sometimes, but there's something else. Every witch has her very own weapon, one that is unique to just that witch. We just have to find yours."

Now Julie felt a little hope breaking into the lump in her chest. If she had something to help her fight, maybe she could do this.

"Really?" Julie said, looking Emerald up and down. Emerald was very old and Julie had a hard time believing Emerald had a weapon. "Let's see yours."

Emerald smiled. "These," she said holding up her hands. Instantly, her fingertips turned to sharp claws. "My claws can cut almost everything and I can climb a tree as fast as a cat."

"Wow," Julie said in awe. She liked the idea that her old witch friend could still climb trees. It made her feel a little bit better. Emerald did look quite scary with those mean claws.

"The problem is," Emerald continued, "a weapon will only first appear when two conditions are met. First, the witch must be very afraid. Second, the witch must have no other way to protect herself from what she fears. My weapon appeared when I was lost in a jungle and a huge slithering snake wrapped around me. Ink and Ice tried to claw at it, but they couldn't get me out. Just as the snake opened its mouth with its sharp fangs to take a bite out of my leg, my claws appeared. I slashed that snake's head right off. Then I cut myself out. I used my claws to climb from tree to tree until I found my way home."

Julie shivered. "That sounds scary."

"It was, but the scariest thing of all was that I was alone. I had Ink and Ice, but I had no other witch to help me. I sat up on a treetop with Ink and Ice curled in my lap and I cried until I couldn't cry anymore. I shouldn't have had to learn about my weapon that way. I want to make sure you don't feel as alone as I did. So today, we find your weapon."

Julie gulped. "Can you just tell me what my weapon is and we can go home?" She felt the panic rising in her chest. "I'm feeling very afraid already. I don't need to feel even more scared."

"No, your weapon only arrives when you need it. The good news is, once your weapon appears for the first time, you can call upon it whenever you want. That way you can practice with it. The sooner you awaken your weapon, the sooner you can practice."

Julie sighed. She wrung her hands together and stared at her feet. "I guess let's get it over with. First though, you have to promise my Symbia will be safe."

Emerald waved her cane and Julie's bag lifted off her shoulder, floated over Emerald's head, and wrapped itself around Emerald.

"Deal," Emerald said.

"Second, you have to promise you won't let me die." Julie tried to make her voice sound strong, but the word "die" caught in her throat and made her lip tremble. She tried to look at Emerald, but her tears had pricked her eyes and so she looked away.

"I promise I won't let you die, but if you don't protect yourself you could get very, very hurt." Emerald didn't even blink when she said it. "You must fight."

Julie flinched. "I understand." Julie's knees started to shake and she balled her hands into fists trying to stop them from shaking too.

Emerald clapped her hands. "Okay, first step is you will pick an animal to fight."

Emerald waved her cane and a cloud appeared in front of them. An image of a lion with red eyes roared as it tore its sharp teeth into a rabbit. Then it morphed into a massive black bird with long talons and a beak so large it could swallow Julie in one bite. Julie trembled. The mist shifted and a six-legged creature with leather skin and a sharp horn on its head took the bird's place. Finally, an enormous spotted cat stalked close to the ground and licked its claws. The sun gleamed off its razor teeth.

As the image faded, Emerald cleared her throat. "These creatures look like animals you may know, but they are like no animals on Earth. They have powers that make them stronger and bigger than their animal forms. They can jump higher, run faster, and kill quicker because they are made of magic. Most importantly, they know your scent and when they appear, they will hunt you. They will not stop until you stop them or you are close to death. I will be here, but you must do this on your own."

"Can I choose the rabbit?" Julie asked, her voice breaking.

"No. Julie, you must choose the animal that will hunt you. There is no getting out of this."

Julie chewed her bottom lip. "I don't want to choose."

"Then I will choose for you."

Julie wrapped her arms around her body. "No," she sighed, "I'll do it."

She shuffled her feet in the dirt trying to stall for more time. She didn't want to choose the bird because it could fly after her in the sky. The animal with leather skin had too many legs. The lion's eyes scared her more than its sharp teeth. She looked out into the field and saw Ink and Ice tumbling together through a patch of dandelions.

"The cat. I want the cat to chase me." Julie tried to sound brave, but her words squeaked out.

"Then I will make it so." Emerald shook her cane and out in the distance Julie saw a small dot of a spotted cat appear. It howled and started to sprint toward her in a blur of legs and fur. It ran faster than any cat Julie had ever seen and it was bigger than a horse carriage.

"You chose the Cheetha," Emerald said, talking quickly. "It is the fastest creature in the world. It has sharp teeth, even sharper claws, and can kill a grown man." By the time Emerald finished, the cat had trotted close enough for Julie to see its big pink tongue rolling over its razor fangs. Its claws kicked up clumps of dirt as it sprinted toward her.

"Emerald, you wouldn't really make something hurt me would you?" Julie asked trembling. "You wouldn't do that to me. I don't believe you'd make me do this. I don't really need to fight."

"Julie, you must fight," Emerald ordered. "This isn't a trick. I put the spell into motion, it only stops if you stop the Cheetha or you are close to death."

Julie's heart thumped so hard it hurt. She sucked in a breath and knew she should run, but nothing happened. She just stood there frozen. Her mind screamed out for her to get away, but her legs refused to move. The cat stalked close to the ground and now stood just a few feet from her. It bared its sharp claws. When it leapt into the air, it growled and then snapped its mouth aiming to tear into Julie's neck. Julie shrieked and threw her arms up to hide her eyes from the snarling beast.

"Today, I will die!" she screamed. She felt the Cheetha's hot breath close to her face as she tumbled to her knees.

CHAPTER 15

Julie heard a zing, a thump and a yelp. Something had shot from her fingers, but she didn't understand what. The cat had slammed into it then rolled on its back into the dirt. Julie opened her eyes and watched the cat shake its head back and forth as if trying to erase the stars from its head. Finally, Julie's feet listened and she leapt up and burst away.

"Julie, you made a shield spell," Emerald called to her as she ran. "A shield isn't your weapon, but it will keep you safe like a bubble around you. It is hard to keep up, but it will serve you."

Julie barely heard Emerald as she sprinted away. Her breath came out loud and her heart thumped as her feet hit the ground with a snap, snap, snap. She sprinted past Ink and Ice. Ink glanced over at Emerald and then his eyes landed on the Cheetha.

"Oh, no!" Ink yowled, "Emerald is making Julie find her weapon!" The cats turned and sprinted at Emerald. "Why didn't she tell us?"

"Because she knows we'd try and stop her," Ice said.

They ran at the Cheetha, but it just leapt over them as if they didn't exist. Its eyes were locked onto Julie.

Julie concentrated on making her legs run as fast as she could. She chanted to herself as she ran, trying hard to keep the panic from freezing her in place again.

"My papa and mama will protect me," she chanted. "I just have to get home."

The field stood so far from her house that it would take her a very long time to get there. She knew in her heart the Cheetha would catch her long before that, but in her panic, it was all she could think to do.

She looked over her shoulder and saw the Cheetha bounding after her. She grabbed her necklace and imagined herself running like the wind. The spell swirled around her, kicking up dust as her legs moved into a blur. She gasped at the energy it took, but she pulled farther ahead of the Cheetha.

"My mama will save me. My papa will save me." Julie repeated.

She could barely keep one thought in her head before another tumbled in. Her thoughts scrambled together making it impossible to really form a plan. She decided to leap into the tree forest next to the field once she reached the trees. "I'll jump from tree to tree until I lose the cat, then I'll fly home."

She looked up at the giant trees and picked the tallest one. She reached the edge of the field and leapt into the air. She stretched out her arm for the closest tree branch, but instead of landing on the tree, she hit something that felt like an invisible wall. She smacked into it and it stretched like bubble gum. It wasn't sticky, but her face sank into it and left nothing for her to grab. She sank deeper. Then the wall sprung back and rocketed her down to the ground like a sling shot.

She landed with a thump as dust rose around her. The gravel and dirt scraped her back and tiny rocks dug into her face.

"What was that?!" she yelled, thinking it might have been part of the tree she hadn't seen as she jumped.

Emerald said something, but Julie couldn't hear through her gasping. She leapt up and ran with all her might into the forest, but again she hit something and her whole body sank into it. It stretched just a bit and then spat her back out. She landed hard, this time scraping her elbow as she slid into the dirt.

Emerald yelled again, "Julie you cannot run! I put a spell on the field to keep you here. You must fight!"

Julie screamed in frustration as the Cheetha came within a few feet of her.

"I'll fly over that wall and find my papa," Julie said just as the cat slowed down, ready for another pounce at her.

She could see the slobber from its mouth. It glared at her with its wild blue eyes. The cat jumped just as Julie rocketed to the sky. The Cheetha's paws were the size of her head and it reached up and slashed at her. Its claws dug into her leg, ripping her skin and tearing off clumps of her shoes. Julie swallowed a scream as she flew higher.

The cat snarled as it landed. It swallowed the bits of fallen shoe in one gulp, then looked for Julie and jumped again. It reached the top of the trees, but Julie had already flown out of its reach. She felt the blood run down her shins, but ignored the throbbing pain.

She flew higher, but then her head bounced off the same invisible wall. She tried to push through it, but her hands pressed into the ceiling and then sprung back. The Cheetha jumped and landed, then snarled and jumped again. Julie flew around trying to find a hole in the ceiling.

"It is no use Julie!" Emerald shouted. "There is no way out. You must fight!"

Emerald leaned on her cane in the center of the field with Ink and Ice next to her. Ice covered her eyes with her paws and burrowed into Ink's fur. Ink wasn't scared; he was furious.

"Emerald!" Ink snarled. "The child is terrified. You must stop this!" He stood on his hind legs and swatted Emerald.

"She must stop it on her own," Emerald said, her eyes locked on Julie. "The spell only stops if Julie fights and wins or she is close to death. Nothing else will save her."

"What if the child has no weapon? Why put her through this?" Ink snapped.

"If she has no weapon, she'll never survive," Emerald said. "If she has no weapon, she will be dead the first time someone tries to steal her magic. She should find out today, so we can stop training her and let her go back to being an ordinary girl."

Despite Julie's frantic flying, she heard Emerald. The words stung. "Emerald would give up on me?" Julie whispered, pushing against the ceiling and trying to use her magic to break the spell. "They don't really believe I can do this." Her stomach flipped. "Maybe I don't have a weapon."

Julie started to send a spell to freeze the cat, but then she felt a bump against her head. The invisible ceiling started pushing against her.

"Stop it!" Julie screamed. "Stop pushing me down!" The pressure collapsed any confidence she had left and she started to sob uncontrollably. She could barely see through her tears. The ceiling kept lowering and pressed her closer to the growling Cheetha.

✳ 111 ✳

"There is no other way out except to fight," Emerald said, but she looked just as scared as Julie.

"You don't think I have a weapon!" Julie cried. Her magic started to fade as she gave up. "I want my papa! I want my mama! Stop this! Help me!" She whimpered. She flew as far as she could from the cat and landed in a patch of wild flowers. Julie made herself invisible, hoping it would give her some time. The cat looked surprised and its eyes darted around looking for her. Then it put its massive nose to the earth and sniffed to find her scent. Within seconds, it found her trail and again ran towards her.

Julie sat down and hugged her knees to her chest curling into a ball. She made a shield, but it took so much energy. She wasn't sure how long she could do it.

"If this doesn't work, I won't have anything else to save me," she sobbed. She let herself appear so Emerald would know where to find her.

The cat bounded at her, then slowly put one paw down at a time, stalking her. It lowered its body, ready to pounce if she ran. Inch by inch it grew closer. Julie pressed her shaking hands into tight fists thinking she could hit the cat until Emerald made it stop.

"Emerald, you promised you wouldn't let me die!" Julie screamed. She tucked her head close to her body and sobbed.

Her body ached and she tried to keep the shield strong. The Cheetha pressed against the shield and growled. Then with its nose, it pushed through it. The shield broke into a million tiny pieces. Julie could think of nothing else to do. She tried to look at the cat, but her tears blurred everything. She wiped her eyes and looked for Emerald. Emerald stood by crying too.

"Fight Little Witch! Fight!" Emerald screamed.

"Stop this!" Ink yelled and clawed at Emerald. His claws ripped into her dress. "I will not stand for this. The girl is terrified!" Ink sprinted at the Cheetha and dove. His claws sunk into the Cheetha's fur and left a jagged scratch on its back. The Cheetha whipped its head around and batted Ink away with one swat. Ink flopped to the ground in a lump of fur in front of the Cheetha's face. The Cheetha licked its sharp fangs and nosed Ink.

"Ink!" Julie screamed and jumped to her feet. She may have given up on herself, but she would not stand for this horrible creature to hurt her friend. "Leave him alone! It's me you want!" She picked up a rock and threw it at the Cheetha slamming it into its nose. She picked up another rock and used a spell to hit the Cheetha even harder in its eye. The Cheetha looked stunned, then turned to stalk toward her.

The Cheetha opened its mouth to bare its fangs. It let out a deep angry growl. In a blink, it lunged. As the Cheetha's paws left the ground, Julie felt her hands humming with magic. She looked down at red angry flames dancing from her hands. Before she could figure out what to do with those flames, the ribbon from her hair untied itself and landed in her left hand. As if someone guided her, she pulled her arm back high over her head. She held on tight and snapped her arm forward. Her ribbon turned into a great whip with fire flames at the edges.

The fiery whip hit the Cheetha's chest. The flames snaked onto the ground around the Cheetha setting the grass ablaze. The Cheetha yelped and fell into the dirt on its back. Without waiting, Julie swung her arm back again, and the whip changed from fire to a long rope. It launched a net and wound itself around the Cheetha's body. The fire spread around them, sending flames high into the sky. Julie flung her arm again and the ribbon changed to water dousing the flames out. The Cheetha thrashed against the ropes. Then with a great yowl, it disappeared. Julie's whip turned back into a ribbon, floated up and tied itself back into her hair.

"You did it!" Emerald yelled, but all Julie could think about was Ink. She ran to him and picked him up in her arms. He lay so still she was afraid he was dead. She let her tears wet his fur and she sobbed telling him how much she loved him. She leaned down to kiss him. Once her lips left his furry face, his eyes fluttered open.

"Little Witch," he said grimacing. "You did it."

"I couldn't have done it without you," she said.

"Yes you could, you just didn't believe in yourself. That magic was within you the whole time, Julie. I just had to show you." He shifted to his side and winced. "Now you see the power we saw in you all along."

Julie brushed clumps of dirt from his whiskers. "I believe you now," she whispered as she gently placed him into her lap. "But right now, I'm only worried about you. Are you okay?"

"Yes, Little Witch. I'm okay," he groaned, but then his face pinched into a smile. "I'll be okay as soon as you promise me one thing."

"Anything my sweet Ink."

"I do believe I've earned ice cream for breakfast."

Julie kissed his head and laughed. "I do believe you have."

CHAPTER 16

After the Cheetha disappeared, it took Emerald a very long time to tend to Julie's wounds. She shook her cane and a magic potion appeared that felt oily, but smelled like cinnamon. The potion stopped the scrapes from burning the moment it touched her skin.

"They'll be better in the morning," Emerald promised as she patted the oil onto the wounds and then wrapped the deep scratches with soft bandages. "You won't even know you were scratched."

"I'll always know," Julie whispered as she hugged Ink to her.

Emerald cast a spell to make new shoes for Julie with two shining emeralds on the toes. The shoes slipped onto Julie's feet and buckled themselves. Julie still sat stunned and just kissed Ink every once in awhile. Julie refused to let him go and tried to calm her racing heart by running her hands through his fur.

"A magic whip," Emerald muttered as she rubbed the oil into Julie's skin. "When I was a child, the old witches told us about a witch who held the powers of a magic whip. I always thought they were lying, because it seemed impossible for a witch to have that much power. A magic whip is an endless weapon in one."

Julie felt too tired to ask questions. She hadn't said much since the Cheetha disappeared. She still felt confused about why Emerald would put her through all that. It took all of her energy just to hold Ink in her arms.

The afternoon had stretched away and the sun faded into a sunset by the time Emerald finished. When she tied the last bandage, Emerald patted Julie's legs and smiled. "As good as new," she said. To Julie, Emerald's voice sounded far too cheery for what they'd all just been through. When

Julie didn't answer, Emerald sighed and dropped her smile.

Julie felt too tired to fly or even stand, so Emerald gathered Julie in her lap to fly home on her broom. Ink curled up against Julie and Ice perched on the broom's straw.

They flew through the cool night and Julie closed her eyes, letting the silence quiet her mind. The full moon helped light their way home and the stars shimmered in the dark. Julie's mother always waited for Julie by the road to their house so they could hold hands and walk together to talk about Julie's day. Julie always came home before dark. Tonight, Julie looked down from the sky and saw her worried mother pacing by the road. It was hours past when she normally came home. Her mother wrung her hands looking frantic with fear. Emerald and Julie floated down like a breeze to her.

Adelaine took one look at her daughter's bandaged legs and pushed Emerald aside to scoop up her exhausted girl into her arms. Julie pressed her face into her mother's body, letting her mother carry her. Julie breathed in her mother's lavender scent, a smell that always made her feel safe.

Julie clung to her mother and started to cry. "Mama," Julie sobbed. "Mama—" Her words choked in her throat and she couldn't say anything more.

"Adelaine, before you—" Emerald started, but Julie's mother raised her hand to quiet her.

"What did you do to her?" Adelaine asked. "You promised she wouldn't get hurt!"

"I'm sorry," Emerald said so softly Julie could barely hear. "I had to teach her to protect herself. She needed to find a weapon—"

"A weapon!" Adelaine spat. "She's ten years old Emerald! Only ten! She has no use for a weapon. She should be able to depend on adults to keep her safe!"

"She is a witch. She needs a weapon," Emerald said and the anger bubbled in her voice. "I had to do it. I had no choice."

"It was not your choice to make!" Adelaine yelled as she helped Julie to stand. Julie leaned into her mother still hugging her tight. "You are not her mother. You scared her. Look at her!" Julie's mother turned Julie to face Emerald. The fierceness in her voice terrified Julie. Emerald glanced at Julie, but then looked away. "I said look at her!" Adelaine repeated through clenched teeth.

Emerald raised her eyes from the ground and stared into Julie's eyes. "Does she look like some sort of warrior to you?"

Emerald stood quiet, then finally shook her head.

"See what you have done?" Adelaine continued. "Was it worth it? Look at the girl you say is the greatest witch to have ever walked the Earth. Does she look like she can take over the world? Or does she look like a scared child?"

The anger in her mother's voice crackled and tears streamed down her face. Julie sent a silent wish to the moon to make the anger float away. A star in the sky twinkled as if it winked in response. Then something caught Julie's attention as it floated down from the sky. Julie blinked and rubbed her eyes. As it floated closer, she strained to make out the details in the moonlight.

"It can't be," she whispered as she saw what she thought was a package wrapped in a red bow. Then as it fluttered down closer, she gasped. Swaying in the wind above her was the promise she made to her mother the first night she learned she was a witch. Julie sighed. That night she'd promised to stop training if it ever got too scary. The package hung for just a breath by her face, then dropped down to her feet and turned into a red seedling sitting on the dirt. The adults were so wrapped up in their argument, they didn't even notice.

"Mama… Emerald… look," Julie said breathless as she pointed at the seed. Neither of the women looked down.

"I will not stand for this," Adelaine was saying. "This training of yours ends today. I will not let you take my daughter somewhere, bruise and scrape her, and return her to me terrified. Julie, I'm sorry. This may be hard for you. But you are not to see Emerald again."

Adelaine grabbed Julie's hand and pulled her to walk away. Julie followed her mother with small weak steps, then stopped to look back at the little red seed. She blinked, and it turned black.

"You will see this is her destiny!" Emerald yelled after them. "You are not a witch. You cannot protect her from all the things in the world that can hurt her. She must learn to do it herself."

Julie watched the little seed turn red again and push itself into the ground.

Emerald stood a bit straighter and when Julie's mother didn't interrupt her, she kept talking.

"Yes, she is very young for these lessons. But just because she is a child doesn't mean she is safe."

Adelaine shook her head. "She deserves to be a child. To play and not worry. Ten is too young to grow up." A sob caught in Adelaine's throat.

The seed stopped pushing into the soil as if it held its breath to wait for what may come.

"She didn't choose this. It chose her," Emerald said gently. "She is the greatest witch I have ever seen. She can help so many people. It is what she was born to do. It should be her choice whether she hides from her destiny or runs to it."

"She won't have to decide because I'll decide for her. She walks away from it." Her mother gulped down her tears. "There is no shame in living a safe life."

Julie stood without moving and the little seed turned black again breaking into pieces.

No," Julie whispered, and the seed pulled itself back together and turned a bright red. "I won't stop." The seed planted itself into the dirt and grew a small leaf the size of her pinkie.

"Julie say goodbye to Emerald," Adelaine said. "You are done as a witch."

When Julie saw the leaf wilt and fall off the plant, Julie gathered up a different kind of courage than what she had used to fight the Cheetha. She squeezed her mother's hand and looked up at her.

"No Mama, I want to keep learning," Julie whispered. Her mother looked down at her with scared frantic eyes. The seedling grew two new leaves, then sprouted to the size of Julie's hand.

Adelaine fell to her knees and grabbed Julie's shoulders searching into Julie's eyes. "You are too young to decide this for yourself. You will understand when you are grown, but some things you must leave for me to decide."

"No Mama," Julie glanced down at the plant, and then looked up to her mother. "Your job is to protect me, but you can't make my magic go away. Somewhere, little girls and boys need my help. I know Cora's life is hard, but you can't keep me from all the bad in the world. No mother can do that. But I can help other kids who don't have a mama like you."

The leaves sprouted flowers and the plant grew to Julie's knee.

Adelaine stood and wrapped her shaking arms around Julie. Julie pressed her ear against her mother and listened to her heart thump.

"Mama, my heart tells me I can't hide from my magic. How can I live knowing kids out there hurt the way we hurt before we found out I was a witch. Please let me learn how to help them."

Adelaine shuttered. Then the plant grew to the size of Julie and finally, Adelaine and Emerald noticed. The plant stretched into yellow, green and blue blooms. Then one flower sprouted soft pink petals the size of waving flags. The flower opened. They all stood for a second before the petals revealed a picture of Adelaine holding Julie as a baby.

"Emerald, what are you doing?" Adelaine huffed an irritated sigh. "Why would you do that? Do you really think a plant can change my mind?"

"I didn't do it," Emerald answered. "This is a Family Bloom. A magic flower sent to tell the story of a family. This flower," she pointed to the picture of Julie as a baby, "shows your past. Soon, another flower will bloom to reveal your family's present. At last, it will give you a glimpse into your future. It holds many truths and only appears when a family desperately needs it."

Another flower sprouted, this time with gigantic purple and orange petals. When it opened, Adelaine gasped.

"It's Cora and Moonbeam!" Adelaine cried with her hands pressed against her cheeks.

The image showed Cora wearing a bright green cloak, riding a silver maned horse along a charred black path. Far away from Cora stood a terrifying castle with black shadows swarming around it. The woman looked just like Adelaine with long brown hair and green eyes. They were identical. Julie had a hard time understanding how her mother knew it was Cora until the woman lifted her sleeve and Julie saw a silver star with shimmers of pink and blue on the inside of her left wrist.

"She's alive," Adelaine said breathless. She hadn't seen her sister in ten years and now reached out to touch the image. But the leaves sighed and then closed.

Emerald stepped closer to the final flower that had just bloomed. "This will show you the future. It may be terrible or it may be great. Prepare yourself for both."

The third flower now opened its dark blue petals. It showed Julie and her mother holding hands as they walked through the doors of that same dark castle. Julie saw herself squeeze her mother's hand two times. As her mother squeezed her hand three times, her cloak lifted just enough to show no star on her left wrist. The castle was dark and Julie's eyes strained to see what lie within. She felt a chill creep around her.

"This is your future," Emerald whispered. "You are together."

In the image, they walked on a huge stone floor with a few torches on the walls lighting their way. They stepped into a grand room. It was bare except for a huge throne where a man with a pointy beard and a gold crown sat staring at them. He wore a black robe and rings on every finger. Dark shadows shifted behind him, but the image was too dark to make out what exactly they were. In the image, Julie and her mother stepped toward him and his mouth curled into a cruel smile. His eyes reminded Julie of the Cheetha right before it tried to kill her. The man held out his hand for Julie to walk toward him. The petals closed just as Julie let go of her mother's hand.

"Mama," Julie said as she wrapped her arms around her mother's waist. "I don't have to live Cora's life because I have you. The flowers show that you will be there to keep me safe." Julie did not understand what she had seen, but she knew it was her future and her mother stood with her.

Adelaine looked down at Julie and shook her head. "Julie, I was there for Cora when she was a child and I couldn't keep her safe."

Emerald stepped forward. "It is written in the stars. It is Julie's destiny, but the Family Bloom shows it is your destiny to be there with her. Before the stars call on her, she must be ready. Someday, she will have to go, but now we know you will be there with her."

"I don't know. It's just—"

"You can't protect your child from all the hurt in the world. You can only make sure she is ready for it."

Adelaine stared at her little girl feeling as if her past collided with her future. When she was a little girl, she swore she'd never let her own child go through what Cora had suffered. Now, here she was feeling as if her daughter's fate slipped through her fingers. She couldn't protect her from it no matter how hard she tried. She shook her head and didn't say anything, but the Family Bloom knew her answer. As she opened her mouth to speak, the branches shot to the sky growing bigger than a house. They sprouted a rainbow of blooms. The roots burrowed into the dirt, pushing deeper and creaking as they threw mud aside. When everything stilled, a stunning tree garden stood before them, waving in the breeze.

Finally, Adelaine spoke. "You may train with Emerald, but I will be there from now on," she said as the branches stretched over them.

Julie hugged tighter to her mama and reached for Emerald's hand. She smiled. "Thank you Mama."

She felt far too weary to say anything else, but her magic glowed from within her to wrap around her mother and Emerald.

Ink and Ice curled up to Julie's feet and rubbed their noses against her.

"We love you Little Witch," Ice called just as Julie's mother picked her up and carried her to bed.

CHAPTER 17

Julie trained even harder in the days to come. Every morning she shook Sam awake and as he lifted his groggy eyelids, she'd whisper, "Good morning Sunshine." He'd jump out of bed and with sleep still stuck to the corner of his eyes, he'd salute her.

"Good morning, Captain Magic," he'd say and then he'd march over to his brothers' beds. "Men," he'd tell them when they finally woke up, "today we fight to make Julie the world's greatest witch."

Jacob and Benjamin would nod their messy bed heads and shuffle to breakfast.

The first time they walked into Emerald's house, Sam and Jacob refused to move and just stared at Madam Doorika. Benjamin held his mama's hand with his thumb in his mouth until he saw Ink. Then he yelled, "Kitty! Give me a kiss Kitty!" and toddled after Ink. He almost tipped over a bookcase trying to reach Ink who had crawled to the highest shelf to escape him.

Another time, Benjamin threw a ball into Emerald's black pot just as Julie started a love potion. The potion exploded into the air and covered the kitchen with purple slime, turning Benjamin almost completely purple. Benjamin ran around yelling, "I love you! I love you! I love you!" as loud as he could until Julie touched her necklace, waved her hand, and the slime disappeared to erase the spell.

When Julie needed quiet to concentrate, her brothers kept busy with Madam Doorika. Madam Doorika kindly let them draw all over her and then erased the marks so they could start again.

Of all the things they did to help Julie train, their favorite was to help her learn to use her weapon.

"Over here," Sam yelled one day from behind a huge boulder.

That morning, Julie had presented her brothers with shields and helmets. The helmets snapped over their faces to protect their eyes from whatever her whip decided to throw at them. The boys had giggled and then promptly slammed their heads together testing them out. Finally they felt like real warriors.

From behind the boulder, Sam and Jacob held their shields and Adelaine hugged Benjamin to her lap. Sam peeked his head from behind the rock and Julie let her whip fly. Out pummeled six banana cream pies that rocketed at him with such force that he covered his head and ducked. Unfortunately for Jacob, he'd chosen just that second to raise his head to see what was taking Julie so long. Three pies splattered into his head, covering his helmet as two more splatted on his chest.

"Not funny," he growled as Julie and her brothers fell to the ground laughing. He tasted a bit of the pie. "Not funny at all, but a little delicious." The siblings roared again and Jacob did a little jig to send the banana cream flying off him.

Emerald pounded her cane onto the ground and clapped her hands. "Alright Julie, enough fun.

We have to prepare you for battle, not a dinner party."

Julie sighed and climbed to her feet to face Emerald. "I hate this part," she mumbled.

Emerald waved her cane and shot thirty tiny pumpkins at Julie. Her brothers cheered as Julie snapped her arm back and the tip of her whip turned to small knives glimmering in the sun. The knives spun at the end of the whip and sliced the pumpkins in half. The knives disappeared as the pumpkins plopped into the grass.

"Very good Little Witch," Emerald said. "Let's see what else you can do."

"Make it shoot rocks!" Sam yelled from their safe hiding place behind the boulder. Emerald held her cane above her head and then twirled it. Out from the ends flew dinner plates flapping with yellow wings. The plates aimed right at Julie's head like a swarm of angry birds. Julie swung her arm back and rocks shot from her whip. The rocks started as pebbles then morphed into fat boulders. The plates shattered into bits, then crumbled to dust.

"Whoop whoop!" shouted Sam from behind the rock. "Nice one Julie!"

Julie smiled, feeling very proud of herself.

"I'm hot," whined Benjamin as he tottered out from behind the rocks and threw down his helmet.

Julie wiped the sweat from her forehead. "It is terribly hot," she said. In the clearing of that field, the sun blazed down on them. Jacob, Sam and Adelaine peeked out from behind the rock and then followed Benjamin.

"I have an idea," Julie smirked as they got closer. "Hold your breath."

"Hold my what?" Sam asked, but before he could ask anything else, Julie pulled her arm back and her whip exploded like a fire hose. It dumped a flood of cool water on their heads. Her brothers squealed as the water sprayed them. Adelaine laughed and tried to wring out her dripping dress. The cats got sprayed just a bit and sulked in the mud until Julie made the wind dry them off.

Ink turned his nose into the air. "It will take me forever to style my fur again," he pouted. He flicked his tail and glared at Julie as he sauntered over to a rock to sulk.

"Oh Ink, don't be such a grump," Emerald scolded.

"I will not join your childish games until I look like a king again," Ink said in his snootiest voice.

Emerald just rolled her eyes. "Alright Julie. What's next?"

Jacob stood up and danced back and forth on his feet. "Make your whip turn into a tornado and shoot me to the sky!" he yelled. Before Adelaine could stop her, Julie swirled her whip around and around, stirring the air. The wind picked up and curled and twisted into a big tornado rolling toward Jacob.

"I'm not happy about this!" Adelaine yelled over the wind just as the tornado started to scoop Jacob up to the sky.

The wind lifted Jacob just a few feet off the ground. He giggled yelling, "More Julie, more! Fly me higher!"

As Jacob rose higher, Adelaine stepped in and finally put a stop to it. The wind quieted and carried him down, but not until he had a little ride around the field like a wind roller coaster.

Jacob laughed and sat breathless on the ground next to Sam.

"It's not fair that Julie gets such a cool weapon when she hates fighting," Sam said as he punched his brother in the arm. Her brothers adored helping her practice, but felt particularly annoyed they couldn't try her weapon. When Sam had tried to grab her whip, it had slipped through his hands like a gooey snake and then turned back into a ribbon to tie to Julie's hair. "We should be able to use it."

Julie shrugged. "I do hate fighting. I wish I could share my whip with you or use my whip to just make people be nice."

Adelaine patted Julie's head. "I'm just happy you've learned to protect yourself," she said. "Think of how far you've come."

Jacob rolled his eyes. "Yeah, remember the marshmallows?"

Julie giggled. When they had first started, her mind kept getting muddled and instead of shooting rocks, she'd shot huge soft heart shaped marshmallows all over the field. She'd blushed a deep red and tried to clean the mess up before her brothers bounced into the pile. But she was too late and her brothers gobbled up the marshmallows, shoving four at a time into their mouths.

"Don't forget about the hotdogs!" Sam said.

Everyone howled. Early in her training, Sam had dressed in a suit made of pillows and tried to sneak up on her. They'd agreed that Julie would hurl tiny arrows that would stick into the pillows. Instead, she rocketed hotdogs at him with such a force it blew him back. She screamed for her whip to stop, but it just kept firing and he practically drowned at the bottom of a hotdog tower until she pulled him out. She'd been so frustrated, she'd thrown her whip to the ground and it took Emerald a day to convince her to try again.

"You've come a long way Little Witch," Emerald said. "Your magic is very strong now."

"I hope so," Julie said as she rubbed her aching shoulder. She picked up her Symbia bag and pulled it over her head as they walked off the field. "I don't think I'll ever have to use this whip, but it sure is fun."

"If you love hotdogs," Sam smirked and punched her in the arm. She shook her head and laughed.

Little did she know that the very next day, she would sprint away from two scary men and a girl named Olive, praying that she remembered everything she'd practiced.

CHAPTER 18

The next morning, Julie's papa and brothers had woken up so sick they couldn't get out of bed, so her mother told her to walk to Emerald's house by herself.

"Just this once my Dear," Adelaine said as she placed a cool cloth against Sam's fevered head.

Julie made a quick potion to soothe their fevers and mixed it into chicken noodle soup. She handed it to her mother.

"I'll be okay Mama," Julie said as she kissed her mother's cheek. Her mother gave her a grateful nod as she took the soup and barely noticed when Julie slipped out the door.

As Julie walked along the road, the sun danced down from the sky and Julie smiled at the freedom she felt walking without her brothers. She loved her family, but they spent every single day together now and she liked feeling grown up as she walked by herself. Every once in awhile she reached down to pat her Symbia.

"You should come see this world," Julie said. "It's full of so much good and I've become so strong."

Julie continued to chatter to her Symbia until the sun slid behind a patch of dark clouds. As she walked past a particularly miserable part of town known for the hooligans that lived within, she saw Olive, the hungry girl from the bakery, standing by a dark alley. Julie met Olive's eyes and then dropped her gaze to the road. There was something about the way Olive slumped against that brick wall that made Julie's stomach flip. Olive still looked just as hungry as she had when Julie last saw her.

"I wonder what happened to the coin purse," Julie muttered to her Symbia. "She shouldn't look this sad after my gift."

Julie walked closer to Olive and tried to convince herself that her uneasy feeling was because she didn't like remembering how hungry she had once felt. Julie should have listened to her worries. She stepped closer to Olive and shuffled her feet against the stone.

"Hi Olive," Julie called when she was a few feet from her. Julie thought it was strange Olive didn't greet her like a friend, but instead glared at her with her arms crossed leaning against the wall. Olive wiped sweat from her forehead.

Thoughts swirled in Julie's mind and urged her to run, but Julie worried she'd look rude to run past her. She should have known her safety was more important than being polite.

In the distance, Julie saw Emerald's alley, but it felt so far away.

"Hey," Olive said just as Julie passed her. "I need your help."

Olive spat the word help and lifted her lip in a snarl. Julie stopped for just a second, then kept walking.

"I'm so very sorry, but I can't help you," Julie said and her voice shook a bit as she said it. "The purse was all I could do for you." Julie quickened her pace. She gulped down the regret that she felt for ever trusting Olive with her magic.

Olive started to walk next to Julie, stomping her feet. "Well my dad took it and spent it on things we didn't need." Olive wiped her running nose on the sleeve of her dress. "So the money stopped appearing. My dad said you cast a wicked spell on our family and we'll have bad luck forever." Olive glared at her and Julie wondered why Olive's father wasn't like her papa. Julie's papa would spend his money on his family to make sure they were taken care of first.

"Well, you would still have the money if he spent it on food for you." Julie said. She wondered what terrible things Olive's father spent the money on to make the purse dry up the coins. "I'm sorry, but that purse was for you, not your dad."

Olive glanced back at the alley and Julie's heart dropped. Something about that look terrified her. Just as she looked over her shoulder, two men ran out from the alley at her.

"That magic purse was wicked," growled the tallest of the men. "We've been watching you, but you always have your mommy with you. Now that you are alone, you must pay for what you did. We'll steal you and force you to make spells for us anytime we want."

The man lunged at Julie. She screamed the biggest scream she could muster and started running. She clutched her Symbia bag to her body as her ribbon untied from her hair. It landed in her hand, but before it could turn into a whip, the man tackled her. Her ribbon snaked around her wrist holding on, but she fell hard on the stone. She felt her elbows and knees scrape against the rock, but even worse, she felt her Symbia bag slip off her shoulder. She watched helpless as it flew through the air. Then her heart sank as she heard it land on the rocks with a sickening crack.

The bag flopped open and her precious egg rolled out. Julie choked out a scream. The fall had splintered her egg with a crack from top to bottom. Tears blurred her eyes. The bad man picked her up and she thrashed against him, but he pressed her arms tight to her sides.

"My SYMBIA!!" Julie yelled, struggling to pull one arm free to send her magic to fix her broken egg. "It will die if I don't help it!"

She sobbed and tried to bite the man holding her. Her ribbon unwound from her wrist and found her hand, but she couldn't get her arm loose to use it. She cried even harder.

"Daddy," Olive said to the man holding Julie. She smirked as she strolled up to them. "I want this witch to be my pet. Thank you for catching her." Olive pinched her lips and glared at Julie. Julie then swung her leg back and kicked Olive's dad in the shin.

"Ow!" he growled and let go just long enough for Julie to dive for her Symbia. Her hand slipped against the egg as the other man grabbed her again and pulled her away from it. Julie thrashed against him, but he held her tight. Olive's dad took slow steps over to the egg and picked it up.

"Is this what you want little girl?" He sneered, his eyes swirling with evil. "Then come and get it!" He laughed such a wicked laugh that Julie knew in her heart what he was about to do.

"Please don't hurt it," Julie begged. The other man held her so tight she could barely breathe. "Please, I beg you. Please don't hurt it."

"I think her wicked coin purse deserves a bit of punishment, don't you Olive?" Olive's dad laughed and Olive smirked. "Why don't we see what kind of powers this little witch has when we break her precious egg."

With those words, the man raised the Symbia over his head and threw it at the ground. Julie tried to scream, but no sound came out. She squeezed her eyes shut waiting for the sound of her Symbia to break against the stones. Instead, she heard another great crack while it twisted in the air. Her eyes fluttered open just in time to see a purple creature flying straight onto the man's face.

"ROAR!!!!" screeched the little creature covering the man's face as he swatted at it trying to pull it off.

"Help me!" he whimpered as he danced around. The creature then opened its mouth full of sharp teeth and took a big bite out of the man's nose. "Yowww!" He howled and fell to his knees.

Olive froze, then turned and sprinted into the alley leaving the two men to fend for themselves.

"A dragon!" Julie cried when she saw the purple dragon with green eyes flying off the man's face. The dragon was so small it could fit into Julie's hands. It roared a bit of fire and flapped toward the man holding Julie.

"It's tiny," the man scoffed. "I'm not afraid of that little thing." With that, the dragon grew and grew and grew until it was so big its huge purple wings swung and hit the man on the side of his head. The force shook Julie loose.

Julie lunged away as the dragon took a deep breath and blasted fire, singeing off the man's hair and eyebrows.

"Help!" howled the men as they tried to run away. Julie pulled her arm back and swung her whip. It turned into a rope and tied itself around the men's feet, dragging them as it wove around their bodies. The whip pulled them into one pile where they whimpered against each other.

The dragon shrank back to its tiny size and flew straight into Julie's pocket.

"You bother me again and my dragon will kill you," Julie said with the fierceness of a warrior.

Olive's dad hung his head. "We promise we won't hurt you," he said. "We'll leave you alone forever. Just make it stop!"

The other man sniveled out a moan and nodded. "We promise," he said. "Just make that dragon go away!"

Julie waved her hand and a sign appeared sticking to Olive's dad's forehead that read, "These men tried to hurt a little girl. Please deliver them to jail."

Then she picked up her bag and sprinted to Emerald's alley without looking back. When she reached the alley, the wind swirled around her and carried her through Madam Doorika so gently it was clear it knew what had just happened. Madam Doorika slammed shut and five different locks appeared. Julie collapsed onto the floor as Madam Doorika clicked the locks closed.

Julie gently pulled her dragon from her pocket, holding it to her chest against her racing heart. She stared down at her and tried to catch her breath. The dragon had sparkling green eyes, the cutest little ears, sharp fangs, and beautiful purple wings.

"My name is Julie," she said running her thumb along the dragon's scales on her back. "Thank you for fighting for me." The dragon closed her little eyes and rubbed her snout against Julie's hand. "What's your name?"

The dragon didn't answer for a bit then let out a little peep that sounded like "Mi." Then she said it again.

"Mimi," Julie said. "What a lovely name. It's very nice to meet you Mimi. I love you very much and I'm so happy you've arrived." Mimi flew up to Julie's cheek and gave her a hot fire kiss.

CHAPTER 19

Emerald heard the commotion from her armchair by the fire and shuffled to the door. When she saw Mimi, her jaw dropped and the book she held slid out of her hands.

"Unbelievable!" Emerald said. "Welcome to the world, little dragon! Julie, a dragon as a Symbia is very special. I don't think I've ever heard of a witch with a dragon. Your magic must love you very much to give you such a grand gift."

Ink and Ice sauntered into the room, but when they saw Mimi they sprinted over and started to fight over who got to nuzzle her first. Mimi spread her tiny wings and gave them both a hug at the same time.

"I knew you were going to be beautiful," Ink purred.

"I knew you were going to be sweet," Ice cooed. "Oh I love you my little kitten!"

Ink tried to push Ice away. "No, Mimi is my dragon kitten," Ink grouched and set about trying to clean Mimi like he would a cat, licking her wings. Ice did too. Mimi let out a "mumpf" but it was a polite mumpf. She let them groom her until it tickled too much and she flapped to Julie's shoulder.

"You'll have plenty of time to get to know her," Julie said, petting Mimi. Mimi yawned and a circle of smoke floated out.

Emerald danced around the room with so much joy she could barely stand it. "Today is the day of Mimi's birth. We must have a birthday party!"

"Yes!" Julie said. "I'll invite my family! I'll send them a Witch-O-Gram."

She touched her necklace and out of the air appeared a pink paper and a glowing blue pen. She sprawled out onto the floor to write her message.

Dear Family,

I hope you feel better. My Symbia arrived! She is amazing! Please come to Emerald's house for a birthday party for her. Please write back if you'll be here. To send the letter, put it back in the envelope, shake it 5 times, and it will fly back to me.

Love and Kisses,
Julie

Madam Doorika unlocked all the locks and opened the door wide. Julie put the letter in its envelope and stuck in the pink pen. She shook it five times and it flew straight out into the air. They waited for just a few minutes before the envelope flew right back to Julie's hands. Julie tore open the envelope and read the note inside.

Julie,

So exciting! Everyone is feeling better thanks to your soup. We're running out the door now. Can't wait to meet your new friend. You worked so hard to grow strong enough for your Symbia to arrive. We are so proud of you!

Love,
Mama

"They are on their way," Julie said, hopping in excitement around the room.

"Well that doesn't give us much time," Emerald said. "Good thing we're witches!"

Emerald winked and Julie giggled. Julie grabbed Emerald's hand and they closed their eyes. In a blink, the entire house was decorated with streamers, glowing candles and a sign that read, "Welcome to the World Mimi!"

"Perfect," Julie said, "just one more thing." She snapped her fingers and set a quick spell to keep her mother from sneezing because of the cats. Then Ink and Ice started to fight again.

"I love Mimi the most," Ink huffed swatting at Ice.

"No I do," Ice snapped.

"No you don't!"

"Yes I do!"

Emerald scooped up Ink and carried him to the couch. "Alright you two, stop fighting. If you promise not to lick her, we'll set Mimi on the couch next to you."

The cats didn't exactly promise, but as Julie carried Mimi to the couch, the cats settled down to make their fluffy tummies a pillow for Mimi.

Mimi nuzzled her face against their thick fur and then settled down for a little nap. Mimi snorted delicate smoke circles as she slept. After all, it was very tiring arriving into the world. All the commotion had exhausted her.

Soon enough, Julie's family arrived and her brothers stormed in, breathless from running all the way to Emerald's house. They galloped into Emerald's living room and looked at Julie, but didn't see Mimi on the couch.

"Where is she Julie?" Sam blurted.

"What is she?" Jacob asked.

"Can she ride on my head?" Benjamin begged.

Julie pressed her finger to her lips for the boys to be quiet, then pointed to her sleeping dragon on the couch.

The boys froze and then at the same time yelled, "A DRAGON!"

Mimi startled awake and flew from the couch to Julie's shoulder. She stared at the boys with her green eyes blinking her long purple eyelashes.

"This is Mimi," Julie said and the boys cheered. Julie's mama and papa gave Julie a big hug.

"We would have been here sooner, but the police were all over the road taking two men to jail," said Adelaine.

Julie sighed. "I'll have to explain to you later about what happened."

Adelaine shot a worried look at Julie. Reluctantly, she said, "Okay, tell me later, but are you in danger now?"

Julie shook her head. "Mimi helped me. But I'm okay now. Let's not let it ruin our fun. Let's have a party!"

The boys cheered again and Mimi flew to Julie's hand so the boys could pet her.

When Mimi smiled, Benjamin shrieked and laughed, "she's a happy dragon!"

Julie clapped her hands and a white cake with strawberry frosting appeared on the table. Julie reached down to cut the cake, but Benjamin stomped his foot and his face scrunched up in anger.

"Mimi needs a candle to blow out!" he cried. "I want her birthday party to be perfect."

He refused to sit down until Julie put a candle on top of the cake. Then he pouted for candles to fill the entire top

"I want Mimi's cake to glow," he whined. Because he was the baby, he got his way and candles soon covered the top.

"Mimi, could you please light the candles?" Julie asked.

Mimi nodded and blew a bit of fire and lit the candles. Adelaine wrapped her arms around Julie while they sang Happy Birthday. After the song ended, Julie tried to explain to Mimi how to blow the candles out, but Mimi kept getting confused and blew out some and lit others with her fire. Finally, Benjamin leaned over and blew them all out.

"That's how you do it Mimi," Benjamin said. "Don't worry, I'll teach you."

As Julie started to slice the cake, Mimi dove her entire body into it. She peeked her frosting covered head out and looked at Julie. "Mi?" she peeped.

Julie giggled. "Well that's not the way to eat a cake. We don't swim in it, we eat it."

The family laughed and Mimi gave off a dragon-sized shrug. She looked a little disappointed until she opened her mouth with all her sharp dragon teeth and chomped off a bite.

"Mmmm," she purred.

✳ 153 ✳

The family roared and Emerald shook her cane and made another cake appear for the family to eat. But before anyone could stop her, Mimi fluttered her frosted wings out of the first cake and took a big bite out of the next one.

"Meep?" She looked at Julie with her cute little eyes wide and batted her eyelashes. Julie smiled and just shook her head. Emerald cut the cake and passed a piece to Mimi. Mimi nibbled at it and smiled. Emerald cut a piece for everyone and even placed plates of cake on the floor for Ink and Ice.

"Symbias love sweets," Emerald said. "Ink and Ice have incredible sweet tooths and it looks like Mimi does too."

Ink and Ice didn't answer, but licked their plates clean, then hopped up onto the table to snuggle against Mimi. After she finished, Mimi curled against them and her sleepy eyes drooped. Julie's brothers helped Julie clean Mimi with a warm washcloth.

"I think we will be happy forever together," Julie whispered to Mimi and then set her in her pocket for a rest.

Unfortunately, happily ever after was the stuff of fairy tales, and life wasn't going to give them happily ever after, not just yet anyway.

Emerald declared Julie an official witch and kissed her. She then promptly gave Julie a few weeks off to get to know Mimi.

"I need the rest anyway," Emerald said. "My back is aching and I haven't had to work this hard in years."

Ink and Ice pouted because they weren't going to see Mimi every day, but Julie promised to come visit.

For the next few weeks, Mimi and Julie spent every second of every day together. Mimi usually woke up first, then murpled in Julie's ear and danced in her hair until Julie pulled herself from her dreams. Then Julie jumped out of bed and slid into the kitchen on sock covered feet with Mimi perched on her shoulder. At breakfast, Mimi ate from her own tiny bowl and always insisted that if Julie had sugar in her oatmeal, she had a sprinkle too. After breakfast, Mimi and Julie would sprint off into the yard and spend the rest of the day soaring together in the sky. They flew to the edge of their town almost every day and sat on a cliff under a ponderosa pine tree pondering what lay beyond their town. When the afternoon stretched the shadows long, they circled back home and always made sure they stayed high enough in the clouds to hide from human eyes.

Mimi's little dragon tongue couldn't make out the words of humans, but Julie didn't mind because she could understand her dragon perfectly. They loved sharing their own language and this tied their bond to each other even tighter.

In Julie's happiness, the terrible fright with Olive and her dad seemed like it had practically never happened. In fact, she felt like nothing bad could ever happen because her magic had grown so strong she felt as if it might burst from every cell of her body. Having Mimi made her feel less alone and filled a space in her heart she hadn't even known existed.

One crisp fall day, Adelaine stood chopping vegetables in the kitchen. She watched through the open window as Julie and Mimi played tag outside in the yard. As she ran, Julie crunched leaves under her feet and her laughter floated back into the kitchen. Adelaine smiled at her daughter's carefree giggles. As Mimi flapped around trying to catch her, Julie sprinted into a patch of sun. Adelaine held her breath as the sun drifted onto her daughter's arms, making her skin glimmer as if it was made of sun rays.

"She's brilliant," Adelaine whispered. She tried to memorize the joy on her daughter's face. She was just about to tell herself that everything was going to be okay, when a black hawk flew through the open window and landed on the table. As it flapped past her, Adelaine thought of the color of death. Cold crept through her as if she'd just walked through a ghost. She shivered, and then swiveled around with the knife clutched in her hand. The hawk held a blood red envelope in its beak. She stood silent and the hawk just blinked back at her.

"Julie?" Adelaine finally called. Julie heard her mother's voice shake and her heart dropped. Their happily ever after had just screeched to a halt.

CHAPTER 20

Julie sprinted into the kitchen with Mimi flapping next to her. She skidded to a stop when she saw the hawk.

"Julie," Adelaine hissed, pointing the knife at the bird. "Were you expecting a visitor?"

Julie shook her head as her ribbon untied from her hair. In a blink, a fire whip sparked in her hand and she held it to her side. Mimi bared her teeth and shrieked, but the hawk still just stared at them.

The bird cocked its head and then opened its mouth dropping the envelope on the table. Julie read her name written in swooping gold script and a chill crept up her spine.

"Someone with magic wrote that and it wasn't Emerald," Adelaine whispered. "I don't like this. On the count of three, you run. Understand? One... Two..."

The bird opened its beak and squawked. "For Julie."

"Three," Adelaine said as she pushed Julie to the door. Before Julie could sprint out, the bird opened its beak again.

"From Cora," it crowed.

They both froze and Adelaine's face turned white. Julie took slow steps to turn back to her mother.

"What do we do?" Julie whispered.

"I'll open it, you stay there," Adelaine ordered and stepped to the table reaching for the envelope. "Just in case, stand by the door. If some terrible spell floats out, you run. Understand?" Adelaine picked up the envelope, but it turned into thick black water, dripped out of her hands, and pooled onto the table. The puddle turned red, then formed back into an envelope. It flew up to the hawk and the bird caught it in its beak.

"For Julie!" the bird said again as it spat the envelope onto the table, "from Cora."

"Prove it," Adelaine said pointing the knife again at the bird.

The hawk pecked at the envelope and the sound of tinkling bells rang through the kitchen.

"Adelaine," a voice said drifting from the envelope.

Adelaine pressed her hands against her mouth and gasped, "that's Cora's voice," she said. She felt dizzy with fear and relief. "She's... she's alive, but she hasn't written in ten years. She must be desperate."

Cora's voice rose from the envelope again. "Adelaine, this is Cora. I know you protect everyone in your life with the fierceness of a lion. I know you would die protecting Julie. The spell on this letter means only Julie can open it. But trust that this is from me. I love you dear sister, and when I say these words you will know I send the letter with love and I speak the truth. I love you from the depths of the sea and around the world too many times to count."

Adelaine shuttered and tears tipped over her lashes. "When we were kids," Adelaine said as she wiped the tears from her cheek, "we used to say that to each other every night before we fell asleep."

Julie grabbed her mother's hand and squeezed it. "Should I open it?"

Adelaine nodded. As Julie let go of her mother's hand, she took scared tiptoe steps closer to the table. When she picked up the envelope, the bells chimed again. With trembling hands, she tore the envelope open. As she pulled the red paper with gold letters out, the envelope disappeared in a puff of smoke.

"That's Cora's handwriting," Adelaine said as she stared over Julie's shoulder at the letter.

Julie cleared her throat to read, but then Cora's voice read the words for her.

Dearest Julie and Adelaine,

Where to begin? I never wrote before because I wanted to do my best to protect you. I put you at great risk just by sending this. I fear someone might follow this hawk out of the land of Acathia and find you. But it is night and I put my trust in the stars.

Adelaine, my sweet twin, I had hoped we would see each other again in a much sweeter time.

But life has not worked out as I expected. I am completely and desperately in need of your help. Ten years ago, I flew to Acathia to help an army of witches and wizards defeat an evil wizard. I thought I would be here for six months, but months turned to years, then years turned into a decade. Still, we have not defeated him. Instead, he grows stronger. This wizard has the name of Dietrick, a heart of a monster and a soul so evil I cry at the thought of it. But more frightening, he is stronger than every witch and wizard I know. My hope, is that he is not stronger than Julie.

We came to Acathia to protect the humans from him. Acathia used to be the most beautiful and lush land anyone had ever seen. But then the Wizard arrived. At first everyone believed him when he said he was kind. Then one day he set the entire countryside ablaze, burning every tree, flower and plant. From then on he tried to control all the humans. Then he started to collect children as his pets. No one has been able to stop him since.

We fought him bravely for many years, but he is too strong. He has won every battle. Now we live in hiding, hoping for something to come along to help us. You see, he captured many witches and wizards and keeps them locked in his dungeon. Our hope is that with Julie's help, we can save our friends, return the children, and defeat him.

I delayed asking for Julie's help for far too long. In fact, it may be too late already, but I must try. Adelaine, I beg you to send Julie to help me. I know she is only a child and you will try to say no. I know you will want to protect her from everything. But do not send her for me, send her for the children he has locked in his castle. Send her because if we do not stop him, his evil will spread. I am sure of it. We need Julie's help to keep all the children in the world safe from his evil. I will do my best to protect her. I put my faith in the stars, and

Adelaine, I ask you to put your faith in the stars too. Julie must fly to her destiny just as I did when I was her age.

Julie, I have no idea if you ever trained as a witch. But the moment you were born, I held you in my arms and knew you were the greatest witch I had ever seen. If you have not trained, please find my friend Emerald, down the 4th alley in town, and knock on her red door. She will do her best to train you how to fly. I will train you when you get here, but I beg you to leave as soon as you can. The journey should take one week. My hope is Emerald will make the journey with you, but she was old when I last saw her ten years ago and I have no idea if she could survive the trip. Follow the map and the hawk will show you the way. I know it may be scary to leave your family, but I did it once and you can do it too. When you get here, you will have me and your new magical family to protect you.

Adelaine, if I were there I would give you wings on your back to fly with her so I could hug you once again. I love you forever. Please do this for me. This letter will now disappear.

With Love,

Cora

When the voice quieted, the edges of the letter curled and burned with an invisible fire that melted into ash. Julie reached down to sweep the ash into a pile, but it patched itself together again and turned into a scroll. She unrolled it and glitter burst from it in a gold cloud. As the cloud settled, the scroll showed a map of the path to Acathia.

It showed a picture of her house and a blinking circle around it that said, "Julie's House." A dotted line snaked from her house, through Julie's town, over a flat land, up and over a mountain, past a jungle, and to the sea. Finally, it ended at a picture of a castle on an island with the word "Acathia." Julie let the map roll shut and it flew into her pocket.

Julie looked up at her mother's ghost white face. Adelaine didn't say anything, but reached over with trembling hands to hug her daughter. Julie curled into her arms fighting her tears.

"I knew this day would come," Adelaine said. "I just prayed it wasn't this soon."

. Julie burrowed her face into her mother's hair and reminded herself to be brave.

"Emerald is too old to go with me," Julie said finally. The words choked her as she tried not to cry. "She can barely make it through a day with me before she has to rest."

"I know," Adelaine said, pressing her hands to her temple. "I know my sweet."

Julie bit the inside of her cheek. "I have Mimi. Maybe that's enough." Even as she said it, she knew it wasn't. Her head slumped onto her mother's shoulder.

Adelaine stiffened and then slammed her fist onto the table. The table rattled and the hawk flapped backwards before landing back in front of them. "How dare she ask for my daughter," Adelaine muttered. "She will not take you. I won't allow it."

"But Mama… they need me."

Adelaine paced back and forth. "My sister is so selfish," she said to herself. "She has the audacity to tell me that she wished she could give me wings to fly. She knows I can't fly! She expects me to sit here and just watch my child leave? What is she thinking?" Her words burned like fire and she kicked a chair. She swung her leg back to kick it again, but then stopped. She lowered her foot and twisted to stare at her daughter. Julie had never seen her mother's eyes look so wild.

"What Mama? What is it?"

"Maybe I can fly," Adelaine whispered. Julie worried the stress and fear had just snapped her mother's mind, making her go mad.

"You can't, Mama. I have to go alone." Julie gulped back her tears.

"No you don't," Adelaine said and grasped Julie's shoulders, digging her fingers into her arms. "The Family Bloom told us I'd be there."

A tiny seed of hope started to burrow into Julie's chest. "Yes, but—"

"I don't know how I'll get there. But remember, while it is your destiny to go, it is mine to be there with you."

Julie's thoughts swirled. "But how?"

"Your magic is only limited by your imagination right?" Adelaine said. "We'll just have to use our imagination. We will do this together Julie. We just have to believe we can do it."

Her voice sounded braver with every word. Julie prayed her mother was right.

CHAPTER 21

The hawk's head swiveled back and forth between Adelaine and Julie watching them in silence. Finally, he sighed and then huffed.

"Okay!" he spat. Instead of squawking, he sounded like a proper gentleman. "I'm not supposed to bring the mother, just Julie."

Julie's and Adelaine's jaws dropped as they stood in stunned silence.

"You can talk like a human!" Julie finally stammered.

"Well of course I can talk," he said rolling his eyes. "I just pretended not to because I wanted to make sure I found the right Julie. My name is Harold and I am a Symbia."

"But where's your witch?" Julie asked furrowing her brow. "I think she needs you."

"You mean my wizard," Harold said. "And yes, he does need me. He is trapped in the Evil Wizard's dungeon deep in that castle. The Wizard stole him just before I left to find you. I've come to gather this little witch to help rescue him." Harold waved his wing and pointed at Julie. "Cora sent me to fetch you. She told me to bring you. She didn't say anything about your mother. So sorry Mama, you aren't coming."

Julie's eyes darted to her mother. Adelaine put her hands on her hips.

"Just one second Harold," Adelaine said. "I won't let—"

Harold shook his head and held up a wing to stop her. "Humans can't fly. Everyone knows that. The Little Witch shouldn't waste her time on wishing you could be there with her. Even if you made it to Acathia, the castle is guarded by Dramins, the most terrifying creatures that have ever existed. They can kill humans with one bite. You'd never survive. You should stay so your daughter doesn't have to watch you get eaten alive."

"No," Adelaine said. "She's not going alone. I won't let her. So you better figure out a way to get me there too." She stared defiantly at Harold and he stared back. Finally, he looked away.

"Humans!" he spat. "You are the most foolish creatures in the world." He sighed. "Very well, if you can figure out how to fly, you are welcome to join us." Then he smirked at the impossible idea.

The map flew out of Julie's pocket and unrolled itself onto the table. They all leaned down to peer at it.

Mimi flew next to Harold. He sniffed and took a step away. "Phew, you smell like dragon."

Mimi snorted at Harold feeling very offended.

"Ignore him," Adelaine said patting Mimi's head. "I think you smell lovely. Alright Harold, tell me. Why can't we ride horses to Acathia?"

"There's no way you can do the journey unless you fly. It would take far too long and I'm not sure you would make it anyway."

Julie's stomach twisted in knots. Harold pointed with his wing at the map.

"The first day we'll just fly over town after town until civilization ends at the edge of the

Plains of Death. No one dares to go there and Cora warned me to never land in it. It's flat and empty with no trees and nowhere to hide. Even worse, ugly creatures with fat horns and terrible faces roam around day and night. They are the ugliest creatures you will ever see."

"Do they eat humans?" Julie asked turning pale. She didn't even realize she'd wrapped her arms around herself.

"I'm not sure," Harold shrugged. "Cora said they do, but I didn't stop." He used his beak to trace the path on the map. "See how the Plains of Death ends right here?" He tapped at a picture of a mountain. "This is Table Rock Volcano, the tallest and widest volcano in the world. There is nothing more terrifying than Table Rock. The steep cliffs and jagged rocks grow vines that will eat you, but the most deadly part is the bubbling lava lake at the top. It bursts wicked flames. No path leads around this volcano. We must fly over it." He shuttered and turned to show his burnt tail feathers. "Cora said the volcano erupts through some pattern, but I couldn't figure it out so I just flew as fast as I could over it. I almost died crossing. No human could get across without flying."

Julie touched Harold's tail and her fingers crumbled bits of charred feathers onto the table.

"I'm sorry you had to go through that, it—" Julie started.

"Never mind my tail," he snapped. He tilted his head and narrowed his eyes to stare at Adelaine. "Now is the time for Adelaine to say she won't risk the journey and she's decided to stay home."

Adelaine rolled her eyes. "I'm not going to say it so don't ask again," she warned. "Now the jungle. What impossible task lies within it?" Adelaine sounded sarcastic, but she wrung her hands with worry.

"The Rainy Forest is a steamy hot jungle with snakes, lions, monkeys and other terrible things swinging through the trees. Cora warned me not to get too close to the ground because most everything eats birds there. We'll follow the river from the sky to the end of the jungle. Finally, at the edge of the sea sits a little town called Waterfare. It is the last town before we fly across the water to the island of Acathia."

Julie's heart sank into her stomach. Julie knew Emerald could never make that journey with her, she was too old. Julie wasn't even sure her mother could make it, even if they found a way to go together.

"Maybe it will just be me and Mimi," Julie said trying to hold her chin up.

"There's got to be a way," Adelaine said as she watched Julie's panic rise. "Don't worry, we'll figure it out."

Harold shrugged. "I've never heard of a witch making a human fly for that long."

"Well you've never met my daughter," Adelaine said pulling her shoulders back and standing up straight. "She's the strongest witch anyone has ever met. She will make it so."

Even Julie heard the worry in her mother's voice.

CHAPTER 22

The very next day, the entire family and Harold tromped into the field to meet Emerald. Julie's papa had not been happy about Harold's arrival and he fought hard to go with Julie instead of Adelaine. But in the end, they put their faith in the Family Bloom and her papa decided to stay home and take care of the boys. The rest of the family wasn't very happy about staying home either.

"I want to come with you Julie," Sam said as they walked to the field. "Please?"

Julie sighed. "I'm sorry Sam, but it just isn't safe. It's not even safe to bring Mama, but I need her."

He crossed his arms over his chest. "Don't you need me?"

Julie nodded. "Of course," she looked at her brother and her heart squeezed. She didn't want to say that he was only a human and couldn't really help her. "I know you can fight but—"

"But, we need someone to help take care of the boys with Papa," Adelaine said, saving Julie from hurting Sam's pride. "We all know Benjamin couldn't make the journey."

As if to prove her point, Benjamin picked up a fist full of mud and shoved it into his mouth.

"Sam, I don't even know if I can bring Mama," Julie whispered, but Adelaine and Sam didn't hear because they both turned to deal with Benjamin who had just thrown himself into the mud crying because they wouldn't let him eat worms.

Emerald stood next to her and patted her back. "Julie," she said, "you should prepare yourself that this might not work. I've never heard of a witch flying with a human for more than a few minutes. Not even in the legends of the great witches does it say it can be done. I think it is impossible."

Julie sighed. "Can you please come with me?" she asked. She knew the answer, but asked anyway.

"No, I'm sorry Little Witch," Emerald said as she leaned on her cane looking very frail. Ink and Ice wove between her feet. "I'm afraid my old body wouldn't make it. But let's try to make your mama fly. At least then we'll know we did our best."

"I will make it so," Julie said trying her best to believe in herself.

So they tried.

At first, Julie used her magic to carry her mother by holding her hands. They floated to the tops of the trees and her mother looked into Julie's eyes and kept laughing, "Careful Julie! Careful!"

They rose up, up, up in the air and did a little turn. But finally they floated right back down like a balloon losing air far too quickly.

Julie collapsed on the ground. "Too heavy," she gasped, resting her head against her curled up knees. "There's no way I could do that for a week."

"Can Mimi carry her?" Sam asked. "Remember how she grew so big?"

Julie's brothers loved the story of Mimi's battle on the day of her birth and often begged for Julie to repeat it at night as their bedtime story. Now, they all turned to Mimi who sat riding on Ink's back like a princess. She just shrugged. Then she batted her purple eyelashes and grew until she was a glorious full sized dragon, kicking up the dust with her flapping wings. She leaned down and let Adelaine climb on her back. Then she fluttered and flapped, tousled and tussled. Finally, she let out a "moop moop moop," as they tumbled over. They never even left the ground.

Adelaine untangled herself from Mimi and stood up. "Thank you for trying," Adelaine said, petting Mimi's head. Mimi shrank to her tiny size and flew into Julie's pocket for a rest.

"What about what Cora said?" Adelaine asked. "Can Julie give me wings?"

"Great idea!" Julie said as she reached up to touch her necklace. She was just about to close her eyes when Emerald slapped her hand.

"Oh dear no!" Emerald said. "Wings are far too painful and take more than a month to grow. Plus, they never go away. Your mother would have wings forever and they would be impossible to hide under clothes. You should ask my Aunt Tipsy. She learned the hard way."

Julie let her hand drop with a sigh.

"What about the wind?" Jacob asked. "It floats us through Emerald's alley. Why can't it help now?"

They all looked to Emerald and she shrugged. "It's worth a try," she said.

So Julie touched her necklace, closed her eyes and tried to conjure up a wind spell that would carry her mother through the sky for days. The wind had a mind of its own and felt quite offended that Julie would ask it to carry a human for that long. It clearly didn't want to help and so it pushed against her spell. Julie asked again. It shoved back, this time blowing Julie's hair into a tangle. She continued to send her magic to poke and prod at the wind trying to force it to listen. The wind lost its temper and with a crack of thunder, pushed a dark raincloud just over Adelaine. Then, to make its feelings clear, it dumped a massive rainstorm over her.

Adelaine tried to run from the cloud, but it followed her around the field until Julie finally yelled, "Okay, I'll stop! I get it! No flying my mother with your help."

The wind huffed an irritated burst as the rain stopped and the cloud disappeared.

"Oh I knew that was going to happen," Emerald sighed. "I just figured you might want to try it yourself."

Julie kept herself from rolling her eyes. "Okay, what about a magical chair?"

This time, when Emerald didn't say anything, Julie asked, "Emerald, what do you think?"

"It's worth a try," Emerald said again with a shrug.

Julie sighed. She made a big soft rose colored chair appear in the dirt. It had a patchwork pattern and soft arms for resting. Adelaine sat down and three ropes instantly appeared, tying themselves around her lap.

"Ready?" Julie asked. She tried to ignore her mother's terrified face.

"Ummm, I guess so." Adelaine gulped.

With a wave of Julie's hand, the chair rose up into the air and started to drift away. Julie giggled as she followed.

"I think we're on to something," Julie called, but then the chair started to get a mind of its own and picked up a bit of speed. "Uh oh,"

Julie muttered as she flew faster trying to keep up. She felt her control over the chair slipping from her magical fingers.

"Uh oh?" Adelaine asked, "what does that—"

Before she had a chance to say anything else, the chair zoomed as fast as it could right into the tops of the trees. The chair stuck there and swayed at the edge of a branch.

Adelaine started to rip at the ropes tied around her, but the chair held her like a stubborn hug.

"Julie?" Adelaine called. "Any ideas?" She teetered at the edge trying to rock the chair back against the tree, but nothing happened.

The wind, still angry about its fight with Julie, decided to send the slightest breeze up to the tree and push the chair out.

Julie screamed as Adelaine plummeted to the earth. Julie tried to press the chair back up to the tree, but it just shook a big no and Adelaine kept falling. Julie flung out her arms and placed the first thing that came to her mind to break her mother's fall. It just happened to be a huge pile of wiggly jello and Adelaine landed into it with a splat. She wasn't hurt, but she was covered from head to toe with red shaking goop. The chair finally untied and spat Adelaine out. She thumped into the dirt.

"I'm too afraid to try anything else!" Adelaine sniffed and plopped her head to rest on her knees.

Julie chewed her bottom lip, trying not to worry. She sat down next to her mother and leaned her head against her shoulder.

"I wish learning to fly was like learning to ride Moonbeam, Cora's Symbia," Adelaine said as she wrapped her arm about Julie. Her body ached from the fall and she wasn't sure if she would ever feel ready to try another idea. "When I first learned to ride, I fell off. But I practiced and then Moonbeam and I soon galloped through the fields together."

"That's it Mama!" Julie jumped up and dusted herself off. "When Emerald brought me to this field, she made a creature appear. It was magic, but it was real too! Why can't we create a flying creature to take us on our trip?"

Their heads swiveled again to Emerald and they all held their breath for her answer.

"I'm not sure," Emerald said thinking. "The creatures I create only last for a few hours. But

Julie is stronger than I am. I've never heard of a witch making a creature last for a week. But then again, I've never seen a witch as strong as Julie."

Harold shook his head and started to pout. He wanted to leave and felt annoyed they even had to pretend Adelaine could come with them.

"It won't work," he said. "That's why witches and wizards who lost their Symbias are terribly evil. They can never make a creature of their own stay. That's what happened to the Evil Wizard Dietrick. He collects children because—"

Adelaine shot Harold a look. "Not in front of the kids," she hissed.

"The other problem," Emerald continued, "is all witch-created animals need something to keep them around. Magic has a mind of its own and it's not something a witch can always plan on. Like the Cheetha, it needed to hunt. Some animals need a certain person always with them. If they don't see that person, they disappear right away. Others need a certain piece of clothing or food. I just don't know what your creature would need. I'm afraid you would be flying when you realized you needed something and the creature would just fade away and you'd fall out of the sky."

Adelaine felt too excited to worry about the details. She brushed the pebbles from her scraped hands and stood up. "Let's talk about what kind of creature Julie should create. We should at least try. Emerald can hold Julie's hand to share her magic right?"

Julie nodded and grabbed Emerald's hand.

"Alright," Adelaine said, "let's list things we think this creature will need."

"Wings!" Jacob yelled first.

"A soft place to sit!" Sam answered.

"Room for Mimi, me and Mama," said Julie.

"Make it big, so it's strong enough to make the journey," added Julie's papa.

"Fuzzy fur to sleep on!" yelled Benjamin. They all laughed until Julie thought about it and it made sense to have a warm place for them to sleep.

"A cover for our heads in case it rains." Adelaine said. Julie nodded.

"It should talk so it doesn't feel lonely!" Jacob added.

"And it should be blue!" squeaked Benjamin, louder than anyone.

As her family yelled out ideas, Julie started to imagine the creature. At first she thought it might look like a horse, but then she imagined long fluffy blue fur that she could burrow against to stay warm and hide from the world. Her imagination grew stronger and she could practically feel the snuggly fur against her hand.

Instead of a horse, it changed in her mind to have floppy ears to pull back to cover her and her mama to block out the rain. She imagined it more like a big fluffy flying dog. She saw a pouch like a kangaroo on the dog's back, near its neck so they could slide into the pouch like a sleeping bag to stay warm and safe on their journey.

She imagined great strong white wings. She made paws to walk through rough gravel. She imagined the creature could talk so it could fly and follow Harold without her having to pay attention at every moment. And she imagined the creature strong. So very strong that it could carry her mama, Julie and Mimi for days. She touched her necklace and squeezed Emerald's hand. Emerald shook her cane. Julie felt the magic pulse around her.

"Bang!" A clap of thunder echoed around them. Julie opened her eyes and saw a giant blue head and soft eyes staring nose to nose with her.

"Well Hellloooo Missss Julie," the creature said. His voice reminded Julie of the flavor of maple syrup. "It sounds like you and your mama need a ride."

Her brothers cheered as they ran up to pet his fluffy blue fur. His legs were massive. Benjamin tried to wrap his arms around one, but couldn't quite get completely around it as he nuzzled into the fur.

"My name is Peppermint," said the dog to no one in particular.

Sam petted a floppy ear. "Nice to meet you," he said.

After giving Sam a wet kiss, Peppermint turned his giant head back to Julie. "I would be proud to help deliver you," he said as he flapped his big white wings. "Oh dear me," he gulped and looked a bit sheepish. "I do believe... hmmm... my tummy seems to... oh dear... stand back... stand back." Julie took a step away, but Sam still stood within inches of Peppermint's face. Suddenly, Peppermint let out the biggest and greatest BLLLARRRBBBBBLLLLEEEE anyone had ever heard. He burped so loud, poor Sam felt his hair fly back as the air hit him.

Peppermint gulped and shook his head. "Oh, please do excuse me," he said politely. "I will tell you that I feel as if I will fade away if I do not have a peppermint at this very moment."

"And so you have it," Emerald said. "Just make sure he has peppermints and he may stick around for awhile."

Julie giggled as she clapped her hands twice. A fistful of peppermints magically appeared in her hand. The kids crowded together taking turns feeding Peppermint the sweets.

"Well if that's the worst thing Peppermint needs, then we'll be okay," Adelaine said as she winked. "I guess we leave at sunset."

Julie swallowed her dread and nodded. "I guess so."

CHAPTER 23

The shadows grew long as the sun sank into the horizon. Julie tried not to look at her family huddled together in front of her. The frost twirled around them, making their breath look like smoke. She chewed the inside of her cheek.

Emerald stood next to her and squeezed Julie's hand. "I hate goodbyes," Emerald said trying to keep herself from crying.

Julie stared from the sunset to the ground, trying to memorize the way the blades of grass looked outside her tiny house. Finally, she turned to her family and shivered.

"I guess it's time to go," she tried to say, but her voice cracked and came out as a sob.

Emerald lifted Julie's chin to look at her. "Little Witch, you are stronger than you think.

Remember that always. You have more courage than you realize."

Julie blinked back her stinging tears and nodded. Then Benjamin sprinted to Julie and wrapped his arms around her legs.

"Don't go Julie," he said, his voice muffled as he burrowed his face into her cloak. He smeared his tears into her dress. Sam walked over and kneeled down.

"Come on little man," he whispered. "Julie's just going on a great adventure. She'll be back soon."

Benjamin looked up and his lip quivered. "But I need her here."

Julie rubbed her palm against his cheek. "Sam's right. I'll be back soon. Some witches need me and as soon as I can come back, I will. Okay?" She tried to sound brave. Benjamin squeezed tighter.

"No, not okay," he mumbled then stuck his thumb in his mouth.

Earlier, Adelaine had hugged her sons for so long her arms ached. Now it was the thought of her empty arms that hurt. She hugged Julie's papa and laid her head on his chest.

"Take care of them," her voice cracked as she pulled away and looked at her sons. "I am not sure when I will return, but I want you all to know that no matter what happens, I love you. I love you for a lifetime and beyond."

Julie kneeled down and unwrapped Benjamin's arms from her leg, treating him like a delicate flower. Then she kissed him on his cheek. He gulped and ran to his papa.

"Sam, Jacob, be good," Julie said. They nodded and she pretended she didn't see Sam crying. Then Julie ran to her papa and he picked her up in his big strong arms.

"I'll miss you Papa," she sighed. He hugged her tighter.

"Remember Julie," he whispered, "if you are scared, think of me. Remember always, that I love you. I would fight for you if I could." He set her down and wiped his tears on the back of his hand. One tear, the color of ice, slipped over his palm and floated into Julie's pocket.

"I love you too," she said. Then she hoisted the magic bag she'd made over her shoulder. The bag would give them food whenever they needed it and held a special pocket filled to the brim with peppermints.

Peppermint leaned down onto his belly to let Julie dig her hands into his fur to climb up. Her mother climbed up next. They curled into Peppermint's sleep sack and pulled the furry blanket up to their laps. Mimi peeked out of Julie's pocket and wiped a tear from her eye with the tip of her wing. Harold flapped up and sat on Peppermint's head.

"Onward Peppermint," ordered Harold. "We must begin the journey."

Julie gulped, but didn't argue. Peppermint stretched out his white wings and flapped them up and down. The wind swirled around her family and the force floated into the garden making the flowers wave a sad goodbye.

When Peppermint lifted off the ground, Julie's papa shouted, "I love you forever!"

"We love you too!" Julie and Adelaine yelled back. Benjamin held his papa's hand and took his thumb out of his mouth to wave goodbye. Julie waved until her family looked like tiny dots below her.

As Julie and her mother soared into the air, the Evil Wizard Dietrick stood in Acathia staring out the only window of his dark castle. A breeze of lavender had just floated around him and his brows furrowed as he tried to figure out why. He looked past the charred ground and tree stumps and glared at the top of the one mountain in Acathia. At its peak, stood the only place on the entire island that grew trees and flowers. Oh, how he hated it. How many times had he tried to burn it? Ten? How many times had he tried to send his magic there to destroy those disgustingly bright flowers and trees? No matter what he tried, they still stood strong. Even now, the orange trees waved in the breeze as if mocking him for not figuring out how to kill them.

Yes, he hated that place because it reminded everyone that something existed that he could not control. He hated that it practically shouted a battle cry that even in the face of evil, life goes on. To make the insult worse, that witch Cora and her followers used it as a safe place to live. He felt his rage bubbling again. His fingers curled around the edge of the window and he ripped off a chunk of the wood.

"What is Cora up to?" he muttered. "Her magic is brewing."

But it wasn't Cora's magic that he felt. It was the magic of a little girl and her mother who decided to believe in themselves and journey to Acathia. He should have taken that breeze of lavender as a warning of what was to come. Instead, he shook his head and dismissed it.

"Whatever it is, I'll kill it," he laughed, because that's what he'd always done. "I'll be ready."

But for some reason, this time it felt different. Finally, his rage and fear erupted and he slammed his fist into the window, shattering glass around him. He stomped away and left the mess for one of the children to clean.

At the same moment, Julie flew above her town, miles and miles from Acathia. But somehow, as the glass exploded, she heard a voice swirl from the wind to her ear.

"Acathia awaits," it whispered, then fluttered on as if it had never happened at all. Julie looked up, but the voice disappeared so quickly, she decided she hadn't heard it.

But yes, dear Julie. Acathia held its breath, waiting for you to arrive.

Acathia awaits

Acknowledgements

This book started as a bedtime story for my daughters because I had tired of stories of girls that needed saving. Then my daughters encouraged me to write it down. My nephew Cole and niece Amelia began to listen too and the story grew to the book that it is today.

Makyla, Aubrey, Cole and Amelia were my inspiration for this story and I would have never finished it if they hadn't given me such encouragement.

This book is also dedicated to my other nieces and nephews: Lainie, Ryder, Asher, Warren, Rocco, Emi, Lulu and Walker. While you live far away or were too little to participate in the process, you are all my inspiration for the magic within.

Thank you also to my husband Justin, my mother Carole, and my Aunt Lynn for their encouragements to dream big.

About the Author

Corinne Magid lives in Colorado with her husband and two daughters. When she's not dreaming of magic, she spends time working as a judge. She plans to publish Julie the Brave, Books 2 and 3 in late 2015. **Visit JulietheBrave.com to learn more about the Julie the Brave series**.

Made in the USA
San Bernardino, CA
15 May 2015